Sports Violence

by Anne Wallace Sharp

LUCENT BOOKS
A part of Gale, Cengage Learning

Detroit • New York • San Francisco • New Haven, Conn • Waterville, Maine • London

GALE
CENGAGE Learning™

LIBRARY OF CONGRESS CATALOGING-IN-PUBLICATION DATA

Sharp, Anne Wallace.
   Sports violence / Anne Wallace Sharp.
      p. cm. -- (Hot topics)
   Summary: "The books in this series objectively and thoughtfully explore topics of political, social, cultural, economic, moral, historical, or environmental importance"-- Provided by publisher.
   Includes bibliographical references and index.
   ISBN 978-1-4205-0625-9 (hardback)
   1. Violence in sports. 2. Aggressiveness. I. Sharp, Anne Wallace.
   II. Title.
   GV706.7.S53 2011
   796--dc22
                                                        2011015525

Lucent Books
27500 Drake Rd.
Farmington Hills, MI 48331

ISBN-13: 978-1-4205-0625-9
ISBN-10: 1-4205-0625-0

Printed in the United States of America
1 2 3 4 5 6 7 15 14 13 12 11

Printed by Bang Printing, Brainerd, MN, 1st Ptg., 08/2011

CONTENTS

FOREWORD

Young people today are bombarded with information. Aside from traditional sources such as newspapers, television, and the radio, they are inundated with a nearly continuous stream of data from electronic media. They send and receive e-mails and instant messages, read and write online "blogs," participate in chat rooms and forums, and surf the Web for hours. This trend is likely to continue. As Patricia Senn Breivik, the former dean of university libraries at Wayne State University in Detroit, has stated, "Information overload will only increase in the future. By 2020, for example, the available body of information is expected to double every 73 days! How will these students find the information they need in this coming tidal wave of information?"

Ironically, this overabundance of information can actually impede efforts to understand complex issues. Whether the topic is abortion, the death penalty, gay rights, or obesity, the deluge of fact and opinion that floods the print and electronic media is overwhelming. The news media report the results of polls and studies that contradict one another. Cable news shows, talk radio programs, and newspaper editorials promote narrow viewpoints and omit facts that challenge their own political biases. The World Wide Web is an electronic minefield where legitimate scholars compete with the postings of ordinary citizens who may or may not be well-informed or capable of reasoned argument. At times, strongly worded testimonials and opinion pieces both in print and electronic media are presented as factual accounts.

Conflicting quotes and statistics can confuse even the most diligent researchers. A good example of this is the question of whether or not the death penalty deters crime. For instance, one study found that murders decreased by nearly one-third when the death penalty was reinstated in New York in 1995. Death penalty supporters cite this finding to support their argument that the existence of the death penalty deters criminals from committing murder. However, another study found that states without the death penalty have murder rates below the national average. This study is cited by opponents of capital punishment, who reject the claim that the death penalty deters murder. Students need context and clear, informed discussion if they are to think critically and make informed decisions.

The Hot Topics series is designed to help young people wade through the glut of fact, opinion, and rhetoric so that they can think critically about controversial issues. Only by reading and thinking critically will they be able to formulate a viewpoint that is not simply the parroted views of others. Each volume of the series focuses on one of today's most pressing social issues and provides a balanced overview of the topic. Carefully crafted narrative, fully documented primary and secondary source quotes, informative sidebars, and study questions all provide excellent starting points for research and discussion. Full-color photographs and charts enhance all volumes in the series. With its many useful features, the Hot Topics series is a valuable resource for young people struggling to understand the pressing issues of the modern era.

A WORLDWIDE PHENOMENON

"Violence," proclaimed political activist H. Rap Brown in 1967, "is as American as cherry pie."[1] Violence, of course, is not a uniquely American phenomenon; every civilization throughout history has had to contend with violence. Violent behavior is also an all-too-common occurrence in modern life. Today's newspapers and television broadcasts contain frequent references to violent acts. Vicious assault, murder, and acts of terrorism monopolize the headlines; violence seems to be everywhere.

Violence has also always been present in the world of sports. Although violent acts are common in a wide variety of sports and across every level of competition, concerns over the frequency, intensity, and potential consequences of sports violence have grown in recent decades. Sociologists, psychologists, and sports theorists all agree that sports violence is a worldwide phenomenon that seems to be growing more and more serious. Dawn Comstock of Ohio State University elaborated in 2006: "Our . . . research studies have shown sports-related violence appears to exist across the board in all sports and seems to be increasing."[2]

Violence is generally defined as the use of physical force to intimidate, injure, or destroy. Authors Lynn M. Jamieson and Thomas J. Orr summarize what happens when sports and violence are combined: "We have the following: contact or non-contact behavior which causes harm [and] occurs outside the rule; . . . [sports violence] has the potential . . . to cause harm or destruction."[3] The long-term effects of sports violence, in fact, are often quite serious to the bodies of athletes from a wide variety of sports.

Many people think of violence as an illegal act, but in sports many levels of violence are perfectly acceptable and often praised. In fact, norms and ethics in sports are very different from norms and ethics in other aspects of culture. Writer Jay Coakley explains: "Athletes are often praised for their extreme actions that risk health and well-being and inflict pain and injury on others, whereas non-athletes would be defined as deviant for doing the same things."[4]

Soccer spectators in Argentina fight during a match. Around the world, fans' enthusiasm for their teams can become heated, often leading to violence.

Furthermore, sports seem to be an area of life where it has become permissible to suspend the usual moral standards the average citizen uses. With moral considerations often set aside during athletic competition, it is not surprising that aggression against other players is often present. Writer John H. Kerr concludes: "Outside of wartime, sport is perhaps the only setting in which acts of interpersonal aggression are not only tolerated but enthusiastically applauded by large segments in society. It is interesting to consider that if the mayhem of the ring or gridiron were to erupt in a shopping mall, criminal charges would inevitably follow."[5]

Despite the seriousness of sports violence, however, sports are today—and always have been—an important part of a country's culture. "America," said U.S. president Bill Clinton in 1998, "is a sports crazy country, and we often see games as a . . . symbol of what we are as a people."[6] Clinton went on to say that sports often reflect all that is good about the American way of life, in particular competitiveness and the capacity for hard work. He, like, many other Americans, believes that sports strengthen character and a sense of community. Other commentators, however, do not share the former president's viewpoint. Writer Viv Saunders expounds: "Some believe sport represents all that . . . [is] bad in the American character—excessive greed, commercialism, violence, drug abuse, and cheating."[7]

Authors Jamieson and Orr contend that sports are one of the ways that we are introduced to a nation and its citizens. They explain:

> Sports is merely a reflection of society, one lens by which we define what that society stands for and creates as an image for itself. . . . It is a positive reflection, for the most part, but the phenomena that surround the violent aspects of sports reveal a great deal of the underbelly of a society's character, and herein, reflect on all of those who participate either directly or indirectly in the sport experience.[8]

Violence in sports exists in nearly every major sport and is present at every level of sports from youth leagues to professional ranks. In addition, sports violence extends to actions other than those taken out on the field of play. Spectators who throw objects on the field or riot and brawl in the stands are a part of sports violence, as is any media reporting of violence that negatively impacts viewers. Sports violence can also include any sports injury that is the result of drug use, any overemphasis on winning that results in emotional damage or physical injury, any off-the-field violence committed by athletes, and any action by sports role models that seems to make violence acceptable.

Authors Jamieson and Orr contend that the world is facing an "epidemic of sport violence . . . that permeates through the entire sport . . . continuum."[9] The difficulty in addressing this rise in violence revolves around the issue of defining acceptable and unacceptable violence.

CHAPTER 1

VIOLENCE IN SPORTS—
SANCTIONED AND
UNSANCTIONED

Violence is present in all contact sports worldwide, from the youth leagues to the professional ones. Most sports experts define sports violence as any act by a player that has the intent to inflict pain or injury to an opponent. The definition does not include injuries that are a "normal" part of the game.

Most experts agree that there are two kinds of sports violence—sanctioned and unsanctioned. Many sports, they explain, such as football, ice hockey, and boxing are inherently violent. Tackling, rough play, and punching are considered normal parts of those sports. While most sports experts consider these acts acceptable, there is also a growing group of sociologists and psychologists who believe that even this normally accepted violence is unwarranted and unhealthy.

The majority of analysts, however, focus their attention on what they consider the second kind of sports violence: the unacceptable or unnecessary. The distinction, however, between senseless violence and the normal rough-and-tumble of play is often hard to make. A player hitting an opponent with a fist, slamming a hockey stick against an opponent's head, purposely delivering a vicious football hit, deliberately ramming another car in a National Association for Stock Car Auto Racing (NASCAR) race, and deliberately throwing a baseball at a batter's head are all examples of unacceptable sports violence.

Violence in sports, both acceptable and unacceptable, receives lots of attention in the media. The media have played their own role in sports violence by making such violence more visible during the last half of the twentieth century. The violence that had always been a part of sports was now being seen for the first time on television by millions of viewers.

Adding to the problem of sports violence is the rising rate of violence in youth sports. Such violence has dramatically increased in youth sports during the last decade. Over 30 million children are involved in some form of youth sports in the United States. The National Alliance for Youth Sports, a Florida-based organization that deals with violence in youth sports, reports on a survey taken in 2001: "[Violence] and abuse occurs at 15% of all youth sporting events, three times more than it did five years ago."[10]

Sports Violence in History

Sports violence is not a new phenomenon. In many ancient societies, the government's primary goal was to conquer neighboring countries, using a vast army of warriors, in order to expand its territory and power. Violence in these cultures was common and often carried over into athletic endeavors. Writer Jonathan Hardcastle elaborates: "During the Roman Empire [for instance] violence in sports became the generally accepted principle and spectators not only endorsed it, but also embraced it as a social norm."[11]

The distinction between senseless violence and accidental contact can be hard to make. Deliberately ramming a car in NASCAR is unacceptable sports violence, but the huge crash involving other cars that results is a common part of racing.

Violence in sports, in fact, dates back at least as far as the ancient gladiators of Rome. Journalist Rit Nosotro explains the role of a gladiator: "A gladiator is a person, usually a professional combatant, a captive, or a slave, trained to entertain the public by engaging in mortal combat with another person or a wild animal in the ancient Roman arena."[12] In order to survive, the gladiator had to be quick, ruthless, and violent.

The first gladiator matches took place in Rome in 264 B.C.; the sport continued, despite the brutalities, for more than six hundred years before being abolished. D.G. Kyle, in his book *Spectacles of Death in Ancient Rome*, elaborates: "Whether it was the arenas, amphitheaters, open fields, and circuses the Romans engaged in their gladiator games, hunts, public executions, and shows with vigor, ingenuity, and enthusiasm. There was simply no widespread opposition to the inhumanity of the game."[13] Thousands of Romans from all classes, in fact, cheered wildly as contestants were gored to death by wild animals—the bloodier the better.

EVEN SANCTIONED VIOLENCE IS NOT ACCEPTABLE IN ICE HOCKEY

"Anything that takes one's eye away from the skill and artistry of the best players in the world in my mind undermines the product."—Mike Wilbon, *Washington Post* journalist, on whether fighting should be eliminated from ice hockey

Quoted in Kevin Quinn. "Violence Has Become a Part of the American Sports Culture." *Marist News Watch*, Spring 2003. www.academic.marist.edu/mwwatch/spring03/articles/Sports/sportsfinal.html.

In addition to gladiator matches, the ancient Greeks and Romans also competed in chariot races in which drivers raced two-wheeled carts that were pulled by horses. Each race generally featured forty chariots that ran the length of a track and then circled back to the starting point. During the course of nearly every event, there were numerous bloody and often fatal accidents as horses and chariots careened into each other. Many of these

During the Roman Empire, violence in sports became a generally accepted practice. Gladiator combat was one of the most violent sports in history.

contests also led to riots and violence among the spectators. For example, in A.D. 532 in Constantinople, a rivalry between the Blue and Green chariot racing teams led to over thirty thousand deaths when a riot broke out during the event.

There were also several other ancient sports that were inherently violent. Boxing, for instance, which dates back five thousand years to early Egypt, was one such sport. Around the same time, the Etruscans in Italy started to include fights in some of their funeral rites, especially for the wealthy. Slaves were forced to fight to the death in front of open coffins to ensure that the departed would enjoy a good afterlife. In addition, the early Aztecs and Mayans of Central America also indulged in a variety of ritual games in which death was common. Tournaments in medieval Europe were often designed as training for war and also had fatal consequences.

Inherent, or Sanctioned, Violence

Violence has also permeated the modern world of athletics. Some kinds of violence have been deemed to be intrinsic to particular sports. These violent acts are said to be sanctioned, acceptable, or "legal." Boxing, for instance, has violence at its core; the sole intent in boxing is to hit an opponent in an effort to incapacitate or injure him and thus win the fight. Football also has built-in violence that involves tackling, an act of violence done with the intention of stopping a player.

Mixed martial arts is another sport in which violence is both sanctioned and expected. Cage fighting, for instance, is a no-holds-barred kind of fighting that includes boxing, wrestling, and various forms of martial arts. The sport is booming despite its many critics who claim the sport is too brutal and bloody. A decade ago, such fighting was barely legal; today it is a fully regulated sport and one of the fastest-growing and most popular televised sports in the world.

On-the-field fighting is not generally an approved action in most sports. In professional ice hockey, however, fighting is viewed as part of the sport. The unwritten rule in hockey is that every player must come to the aid of a teammate who is bullied, hit, or suffering an injury because of a hard hit. Likewise, when fights break out, these players must honor this so-called buddy system and join in the melee. Furthermore, hockey officials and management are reluctant to ban fighting because both players and fans seem to expect and enjoy it.

One of the reasons such acts of violence are allowed in these sports is that the participants have agreed beforehand that these acts are an acceptable part of that particular sport. Written rules have been put into place to prevent other forms of violence from occurring. Referees and umpires are then hired to ensure that the athletes do not act in opposition to the rules. Football players thus agree that tackling is an approved act; cheap shots—violent actions that aim to deliberately hurt an opponent—are not. Penalties are then imposed for those players acting in an unapproved manner.

The Enforcer

Ice hockey has a long history of violence, both sanctioned and unsanctioned. For years many teams employed a player who was referred to as the "enforcer" or "goon." These players seldom scored but could be counted on to initiate fights in the hopes of changing a game's momentum. It was the enforcer's job to intimidate opposing players and use violence to deter the other team. The enforcer usually left his opponent unconscious on the ice.

The National Hockey League began to curtail this kind of behavior in the 1980s. Concerned about not having a national television contract because of the violence, the league was hoping to improve its image. Officials began severely penalizing players who initiated fights. By the late 1990s hockey had cleaned up its act; teams that had once employed several enforcers were down to one. The number of fights decreased dramatically.

Many of the toughest players, however, continue to be fan favorites. Coaches, however, are less tolerant of such antics, especially during playoff games. When the end of the season comes around, many of the enforcers are not on the ice; the team cannot afford to take unnecessary penalties that would give the other team an advantage on the ice.

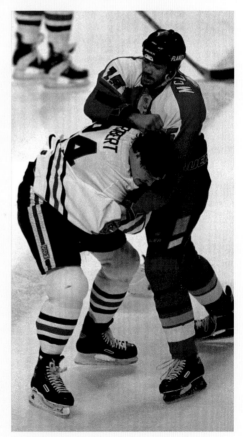

Enforcers fight during a National Hockey League match. An enforcer's job is to rattle and intimidate the opposing team through the use of physical force

While aggressive play is expected and rewarded, the majority of players try to draw a line between acceptable and unacceptable aggression. In baseball, sliding hard into second base to break up a double play, for instance, is acceptable, while leaving the base path to intentionally knock down a fielder is not. Rushing a quarterback and tackling him before he throws the ball is an acceptable form of violence in football; hitting the quarterback after he has released the ball is not acceptable.

SANCTIONED VIOLENCE IS PERFECTLY ACCEPTABLE

"Sanctioned aggression and violence in sport is an inherent, enjoyable aspect of play in . . . team sports. It should, therefore, not be objectionable, and neither should reading about or viewing sanctioned aggression and violence in the media be problematic."—John H. Kerr, author of *Rethinking Aggression and Violence in Sport*

John H. Kerr. *Rethinking Aggression and Violence in Sport.* London: Routledge, 2005, p. 129.

Despite the many safeguards that have been built into the world of sports, even sanctioned violence has its risks. Even normal and acceptable forms of violence take an enormous toll on a player's body. In fact, 90 percent of all injuries occur as a result of sanctioned types of violent contact.

Despite the potential for injury, many athletes find sanctioned violence and aggression both satisfying and pleasurable. Problems occur, however, when the fine line is crossed into unsanctioned violence.

Unsanctioned Violence

The line between sanctioned and unsanctioned violence is not always very clear. Writer A. Brink explains the difference between the two kinds of violence: "The distinction between hard play and foul play lies in the resort of the latter to violence of [the] underhand[ed], malicious, [and] treacherous kind."[14]

Proportion of Injuries in High School Sports Practices and Competitions, by Diagnosis, 2005–2006

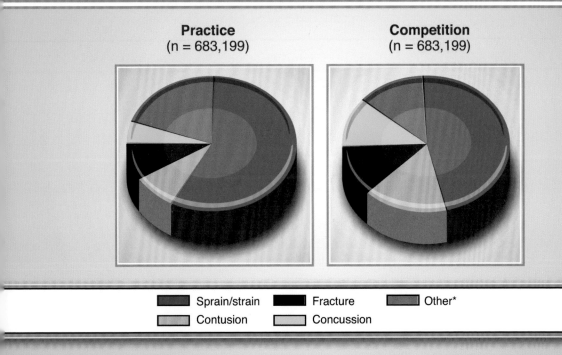

Practice
(n = 683,199)

Competition
(n = 683,199)

Legend:
- Sprain/strain
- Contusion
- Fracture
- Concussion
- Other*

*Includes other injuries (e.g., lacerations or dislocations) and reportable health-related events (e.g., heat illness, skin infections, or asthma attacks).

Taken from: www.cdc.gov/mmwr/preview/mmwrhtml/mm5538a1.htm.

Unsanctioned violence is any violent act outside the written and unwritten rules of a particular sport. Unwritten rules, for example, include the unspoken agreement among teammates that an athlete does not allow himself or a teammate to be unfairly brutalized by the opposing team without retaliating in kind.

Part of the reason for so many acts of unsanctioned violence is that most athletes tend to think of the opposing team as the enemy. By thinking in this way, the use of violence to interfere with an opposing player's performance becomes acceptable behavior. In any other area of life, these same athletes might consider such acts as immoral, but in sports, they believe anything goes as long as it helps to win the game. The Josephson Institute, a nonprofit group dedicated to improving the ethical quality of society, elaborates: "Separating personal ethics on . . . [the] field can cause decent people to justify doing things during a game that they would never do at home."[15]

Intimidation and cheap shots have become the backbone of many professional sports. A player hitting an opponent with a closed fist, driving a helmet into somebody's head or body, and slamming a hockey stick across a rival's back are all examples of unsanctioned violence. Some players have come to equate excellence in their sport with such violence; these players often use such acts of violence to prove themselves to coaches and management.

Unsanctioned violence also includes deliberately injuring an opponent in an effort to remove that player from the game. Many players, in fact, are best known for such acts of violence. Alex Karras, a former Detroit Lions defensive football player, was one such player. Karras once stated: "I had a license to kill for sixty minutes a week. My opponents were all fair game and when I got off the field, I had no regrets."[16]

Cheap shots and even rigorous tackling tragically result in frequent injuries. The statistics are staggering. The Centers for Disease Control and Prevention keeps statistics on sports injuries. Between 2005 and 2006, out of 7.2 million high schoolers involved in sports, 2 million suffered injuries directly related to their athletic endeavor. In addition, the National Collegiate Athletic Association (NCAA) contends that football in many cases produces more catastrophic injuries than most other sports. The NCAA estimates that around thirty college and high school players become paraplegics—paralyzed from the waist down—each year. With injuries so common, the average playing career for professional football players lasts only four years, making a football career the shortest of all professional sports.

How Unsanctioned Violence Differs in Various Sports

While only a handful of sports are inherently violent, nearly all sports include some form of unsanctioned violence. The form

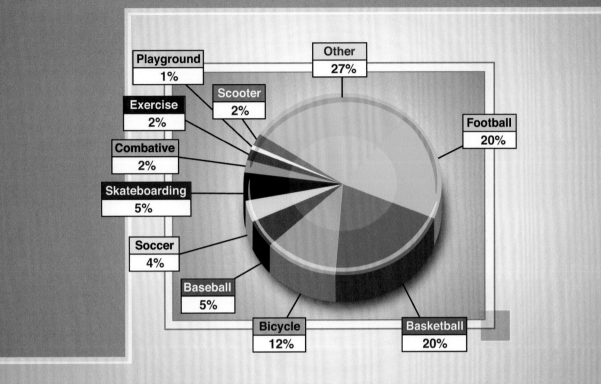

Percentage of Nonfatal Sports- and Recreation-Related Injuries Among U.S. Boys, Aged Ten to Nineteen, July 2000–June 2001

Playground 1%

Other 27%

Scooter 2%

Exercise 2%

Football 20%

Combative 2%

Skateboarding 5%

Soccer 4%

Baseball 5%

Bicycle 12%

Basketball 20%

Taken from: University of North Carolina Injury Prevention Research Center. www.1prc.unc.edu.stats_sports.shtml.

that violence takes, however, differs from sport to sport. Football, for instance, is one of the most violent of all sports, and yet it ranks as one of the most popular as well. Cheap shots are not uncommon in professional football and have been classified as unsanctioned violence. These actions include such things as hitting another player with fists, kicking a player while down, using one's helmet to hit another player, gouging another player's eyes, and utilizing blind-side hits, in which a player deliberately hits or tackles an opponent who is up in the air catching a ball or has his back turned while passing. Cheap shots all too frequently end with injuries for the unsuspecting victim. Many football players, however, believe that such violence is just part of the game.

Victims of cheap shots may have other opinions. During a preseason game in 1978, Darryl Stingley, a wide receiver for the New England Patriots, went high in the air to catch a pass; he missed the ball. Jack Tatum, nicknamed "The Assassin," slammed into Stingley while he was midair and belted him in the head with a padded forearm. The blow broke Stingley's neck and turned the twenty-six-year-old into a quadriplegic, paralyzed from the neck down. Football officials did not call a penalty, nor did Tatum ever offer a formal apology, despite once stating that his best hits bordered on felonious assault. Stingley, like many other players severely injured from such hits, believed that cheap shots had no place in professional football.

VIOLENCE AND RISK ARE A NORMAL PART OF BOXING

"There is risk involved in boxing, as in all sports in which physical contact is involved. . . . To remove all the risk would be turning boxing into something quite different than the sport as we know it—and I do not think anyone would want that, least of all the boxers themselves."—Graham Houston, journalist and editor of *Boxing Monthly*

Graham Houston. "Death in the Ring Has Long Been a Part of Boxing." ESPN.com, November 13, 2007. http://sports.espn.go.com/sports/boxing/news/story?id=3105556.

Those who play college football also commit acts of unsanctioned violence. A total of twelve Clemson University and University of South Carolina football players, for example, were suspended one game after a brawl broke out in November 2004. Clemson senior player Yusef Kelley was seen kicking a South Carolina player who was lying facedown with his helmet off. Both sidelines cleared as all the players rushed to the field. The NCAA acted quickly in suspending many of the players, stating that the athletes had violated the rules of good sportsmanship.

Other sports also see their own share of unsanctioned violence. Sanctioned violence, for instance, has always been a part of ice hockey. Pushing, grappling, and punching matches take place all the time. More serious, however, are unsanctioned incidents in which faces are split open by hockey skate blades, heads are smashed by a hockey stick, and blind hits are made that often incapacitate or severely injure another player. Players, even in today's game where they are protected by helmets and other equipment, continue to have their jaws broken and their teeth knocked out; they also suffer concussions and paralysis. Even in youth hockey, players are sometimes taught and encouraged to fight if provoked by another player; some children are even told to retaliate with their sticks and their fists.

Baylor University's Brittney Griner, right, was suspended for two games after throwing a punch that broke an opponent's nose. The NCAA was criticized for giving her a relatively minor suspension.

Basketball is another sport with the potential for unsanctioned forms of violence. In the beginning days of basketball, however, its inventor, James A. Naismith, did not envision the sport as being violent; in fact, he wanted above all else to avoid physical contact. Knowing that players might get rough, however, Naismith devised penalties for tripping and other contact fouls, all forms of accidental violence. As basketball grew in popularity and became a professional sport, however, the stakes grew higher, with salaries climbing into the millions. With so much at stake, the game became more physical and more violent, with more unsanctioned violence such as pushing, shoving, and flagrant fouls, like hitting a player while he is in the air or punching. This is true not just at the professional level but in college and high school events as well.

In March 2010, for instance, Baylor University's star female basketball player, Brittney Griner, was suspended for two games after throwing a punch that broke an opponent's nose. Sean Mc-Clelland of the *Dayton Daily News* elaborates: "This was a sucker punch, a resounded right hand that broke the nose of Texas Tech women's basketball player Jordan Barncastle, who may require surgery."[17] After learning Griner had received only a minor suspension, McClelland opined: "Guess cold-cocking [knocking unconscious] an unsuspecting opponent just isn't that serious of an offense these days. Makes you wonder what would have earned Griner more time off the court. Producing a weapon of some kind?"[18]

Less unsanctioned violence occurs in baseball than the other major sports. Writers Robert M. Gorman and David Weeks elaborate: "When one thinks of baseball, rarely do thoughts of tragedy come to mind. It is a game associated with warm, sunny days and leisurely outings to the local ballpark. Yet injury and death have been associated with the game from the beginning."[19] The most common unsanctioned violent act in baseball is the pitcher throwing a beanball, a ball intentionally aimed at the hitter's head. While it is deemed acceptable to brush back, or throw a pitch close to the batter to "brush" him away from his normal stance, it is not permissible actually to hit the batter. Severe injuries such as concussion and even death have occurred

The Punch

One of the most notorious incidents of unsanctioned violence in professional basketball occurred on December 9, 1977. The media has since referred to the incident as "The Punch." Sports author John Feinstein elaborates: "It was a watershed moment in sports, because it has become the symbol of what can happen when fights break out among very strong, very athletic young men."[1]

In a game between the Los Angeles Lakers and the Houston Rockets, a melee broke out on the floor involving the Lakers' star center, Kareem Abdul-Jabbar, and one of the Rockets' players. Kermit Washington, one of Abdul-Jabbar's teammates, came to his assistance. Out of the corner of his eye, Washington saw a Rocket player running full speed toward the fight. Reacting instantaneously, Washington threw a punch at the oncoming player, Rudy Tomjanovich, catching Tomjanovich on the jaw and face. Tomjanovich appeared to fly backward before landing unconscious on the floor, blood streaming out of his nose. The punch had landed with such devastating force that everyone in the arena had heard the sound of bones breaking.

Paul Toffel, the doctor who later saw Tomjanovich in the hospital, likened the injuries "to those suffered by someone thrown through the windshield of a car traveling 50 mph."[2] X-rays showed extensive injuries to the face, nose, and jaw. The top part of Tomjanovich's skull was actually out of alignment creating a situation that could easily have been fatal. He later had a total of five surgeries to repair the damage.

Both men returned to basketball but were never the same. Their play suffered, as did Washington's reputation. As a result of the incident, the National Basketball Association increased fines for fighting and also began issuing longer suspensions for such behavior. The league also added a third official to referee each game in hopes of stopping violent behavior before it reached the stage of actual punches being thrown.

1. John Feinstein. *The Punch*. New York: Back Bay, 2002, p. xiv.
2. Quoted in Feinstein. *The Punch*, p. 6.

as a result of hitting a player in the head with the ball. Another form of unsanctioned violence involves running into opponents and deliberately using the spikes on one's shoes to disable them.

While most of the violence seen in boxing is sanctioned and considered part of the sport, there have been numerous incidents in which the violence shifted into the unsanctioned variety. One of the most well-known incidents involved former heavyweight champion Mike Tyson. Tyson, while praised for his ferocious boxing style, was even better known for his controversial behavior out of the ring. In 1992, for instance, he had been tried and convicted of sexual assault and rape, serving three years in prison for his crime. Following his release, Tyson attempted a comeback. Part of that comeback involved a fight for the heavyweight title with Evander Holyfield. During the fight, Tyson was disqualified for biting off part of Holyfield's ear and spitting it on the mat. As a result of this incident, his boxing license was rescinded and he eventually retired from boxing.

Automobile racing, too, has always been a dangerous and violent sport; deaths and injuries are common. With extremely powerful cars racing at speeds over 200 miles per hour (322kph) on a comparatively small surface and track, it is not unusual for the cars to spin out, hit walls, burn, and come apart. What is alarming to many sports experts today is that race-car drivers are now intentionally bumping other drivers with their cars, escalating the violence along with the risk of death and injury.

The common factor in all of these instances of sports violence is that each action is an example of unsanctioned violence. Such acts have become, in many cases, everyday occurrences in sports.

The Role of the Media

Many sports experts partially blame the media for the rise of unsanctioned violence in sports. "If it bleeds, it leads," goes the old television saying. Fred Engh, president of the National Alliance for Youth Sports, explains: "The media are often criticized for leading their telecasts with footage of the latest fight, argument, or scandal."[20] Most sports commentators and analysts argue that television is simply giving the public what it wants. They believe that if the public did not want to see such violence, they would not watch it.

Studies in television viewership support this contention; viewer ratings are higher than ever before for sporting events. Engh elaborates: "Especially in this era driven by ratings, the story has become not about who hit a ninth-inning homer last night, but who purposely hit another player with a pitch to ignite a bench-clearing brawl."[21] Author John H. Kerr agrees and adds: "Writers and commentators often concentrate on these latter, unsavory aspects of aggression and violence in sport, rarely focusing on the positive side."[22] The media, whether newspapers or television, portray sports in entertaining ways in order to earn high approval ratings and readership or viewership. This can result in a depiction that is skewed to present the most entertaining material—and often the most entertaining is also the most violent. Most adults realize this and can easily determine that what is being written or shown is not the whole story; some young people may be unable to separate the fact from the fiction.

BOXING SHOULD BE BANNED

"When the surest way to win (a sporting event) is by damaging the opponent's brain, and this becomes the standard procedure, the sport is morally wrong."—George D. Lundberg, a member of the American Medical Association

George D. Lundberg. "Boxing Should Be Banned in Civilized Countries." *Journal of the American Medical Association*, May 9, 1986, p. 2483.

Those analysts who disagree with the notion that the media negatively influence violence in sports contend that violent behavior is all around us and that it is just another part of sports. They further assert that violence has not increased in the television era. These analysts insist that violence predated the era of television. Jonathan Freedman of the University of Toronto concludes: "The scientific evidence does not show that watching violence either produces violence in people, or desensitizes them to it."[23]

Furthermore, many sports analysts contend that sports telecasts of violence on the field of action actually provide a diversion from the violence that is prevalent in the rest of society. They believe that these telecasts provide a healthy discharge of the viewers' frustrations and aggressions. Millions of people, these analysts state, find that watching sports and the violence that is inherent in such events actually provides a needed release for the tensions and resentments of daily life. A survey taken in 1987, for instance, when professional football was off the airwaves because of a players' strike, showed that some families experienced more domestic violence. Some analysts concluded that this increase in domestic violence was directly related to the absence of football.

Recent Increases in Youth Violence in Sports

One of the most critical complaints by those people who claim that the media focus too much on sports violence is that such violence is damaging to today's youth. Millions of children and young adults watch sports on television. Psychological research has shown that young children model their behavior and attitudes on those of adults, particularly people they admire, such as sports stars. When children see their favorite sports stars committing violent acts both on and off the field, they can easily become confused. Most know that such violent acts are disapproved of by society under normal circumstances, and yet they also see such acts being praised and repeatedly replayed on television. All too many young people then imitate violent athletes when they play informal games and organized youth sports. University of Michigan professor L. Rowell Huesmann elaborates: "Fifty years of evidence show that exposure to media violence causes children to behave more aggressively."[24] They see a football lineman make a vicious tackle on an unsuspecting opponent and may believe that this kind of unsanctioned behavior is acceptable.

A 1996 study by the University of North Carolina reported that an increasing number of young athletes identified violence as a normal part of sports. While the study did not make a distinction between sanctioned or unsanctioned violence, it is the latter kind of violence that most concerns sports experts. Whether the young person learned unsanctioned violence from coaches, from viewing violent television sports, or elsewhere, the impact of the acceptance of violence is evident in the number and severity of acts of violence being committed by young athletes. In August 2000, for instance, a teenage ice hockey player pleaded guilty

Many young people see professional football players make vicious tackles, which may lead them to believe that such behavior is acceptable.

to charges that he had given a rival player a paralyzing injury. In 2005 a thirteen-year-old baseball player killed a fifteen-year-old player in Florida when he struck him over the head with a bat. In addition, a seventeen-year-old hockey player in Canada was charged with assault after purposely spearing another player with his stick. The victim took the blow in the abdomen and ended up in surgery for a ruptured bowel; he missed one month of school and lost 22 pounds (10kg). The perpetrator was suspended for the remainder of the season. In addition to these examples, numerous other violent incidents have occurred. ABC News journalists Michael S. James and Tracy Ziemer explain: "Waves of head-butting, elbowing, and fighting have been reported at youth sporting events across the country."[25]

Some sociologists and psychologists believe that adding to the problem of violence in youth sports is the fact that a number of parents are putting too much pressure on their children to perform or win. Some children have schedules for sports that include practices early in the morning and late at night, practice every day after school, and competition several times a week. This allows little time for homework or time with the family. Writers Lynn M. Jamieson and Thomas J. Orr elaborate: "The all-time pursuit of that elusive scholarship, success, and improved status and reputation seems to be overwhelming and all-encompassing."[26] This pressure from parents can sometimes cause children to play more aggressively and act in a violent way in order to impress the parent and succeed.

With a rise in violence of all kinds at all levels of sports, experts in the field are now increasingly looking for the reasons such violence occurs. They are also examining the relationship between aggression and competition as it relates to violence in sports.

FOSTERING VIOLENCE THROUGH COMPETITION AND AGGRESSION

Competitive sports feature one player or team of players in action against another athlete or group of athletes. The purpose of competition is simple: to win. Winning is an extremely important component of all athletic endeavors. In order to win, players seek to improve their skills and become the best possible athlete. Writers Lynn M. Jamieson and Thomas J. Orr elaborate: "Athletes at a young age are taught to strive for team and personal distinction. In order to reach some type of distinction, an athlete must display skill, dominate an opponent, or do something better than everyone else."[27]

The increased use of violence, both sanctioned and unsanctioned, in contact sports goes hand in hand with the goal of succeeding and winning. In many cases this violence has been taken to the extreme at the cost of sportsmanship, the practice of playing by the rules and exhibiting fairness whether winning or losing. Furthermore, athletes are being taught to make sacrifices as they are increasingly encouraged to play through pain and injury and to limit the amount of weakness they show. They are taught to accept no limits in attaining success. This pressure to succeed can come from many sources: coaches, fans, management, and from within themselves, as well. And while winning and succeeding can make a player's actions and sacrifices seem worthwhile, the failure to do so can produce feelings of frustration and rage, which can lead to more violence.

Some sociologists and psychologists believe that young athletes learn about aggression and violence early in their athletic careers and are conditioned to develop aggressive behaviors. Author John H. Kerr explains that when young players first become involved in a team contact sport, they find that they enjoy the activity; as they continue to play, the level of physicality and aggression usually increases. As more time passes, the physical domination of opposing athletes becomes crucial to team success. The players learn that violent and aggressive acts are often rewarded by praise from coaches, fans, and other players. Eventually, according to Kerr, an "excessive appetite for . . . violence in a team sport becomes the major source of pleasure in an athlete's life."[28]

The Role of Aggression and Intimidation in Sports

Aggression is a form of violence in which a person uses force to attack another individual, while intimidation, also an act of violence, includes the use of words, gestures, and actions that threaten violence. Like acts of aggression, intimidation is used to dominate or control another person. Both aggression and intimidation are inherent in sports and are considered sanctioned acts, as long as the line between acceptable and unacceptable violence is not crossed. Author Kerr elaborates: "The truth is that much of the pleasure, satisfaction, and enjoyment to be gained in team contact sports is associated with the intense physicality. . . . In team contact sports, the element of physical aggression is one of the essential components of success as a team. Physical domination of the opposition by what is often called 'controlled aggression' is a recognized tactic."[29]

One of the big questions about sports violence relates to whether sports provide a positive outlet for aggression or whether they actually increase the propensity for aggression off the field and in other areas of life. Some psychologists believe that any vigorous activity provides a benefit by releasing pent-up emotions; thus, competitive sports provide an outlet through which aggressive tendencies are released. Other sports experts challenge this, believing instead that rather than benefiting the athlete, participating in aggressive sports often makes players act even more aggressively.

Intimidation in sports involves the use of words, gestures, and actions that threaten physical violence.

Aggressive and violent actions on the field also have the potential to impact spectators. The Canadian Centres for Teaching Peace elaborates: "Increased spectator violence is one more manifestation of the escalation of violence which has taken place in our society. . . . Violence between athletes can only serve to encourage it."[30]

Winning Is All That Matters

The use of aggression and intimidation is an important component of a winning team. In fact, the pressure placed on athletes to win is incredible. It comes from many sources: a player's desire to win, a sports franchise's expectation of winning teams, a coach's demands, and fans wanting their teams to be champions.

The need to win was most clearly expressed by legendary Green Bay Packers football coach Vince Lombardi: "Winning isn't everything. It's the only thing."[31] As a result, inhibitions are sometimes put aside in an effort to win at any cost. If violence is needed to earn a win, then so be it. Coaches and other

Tonya Harding pleads guilty in court to her part in the assault on skater Nancy Kerrigan. Harding was sentenced to three years' probation, while Kerrigan earned the Olympic silver medal.

players may even reject and ridicule team members who fail to use violence to gain an edge.

Individual athletes sometimes take winning so seriously that competitors are intentionally injured. In one high-profile incident, for example, figure skater and Olympic favorite Nancy Kerrigan was assaulted after a practice session in a Detroit arena. Kerrigan was hit across the right leg and knee by a man who later claimed he was hired by rival skater Tonya Harding's ex-husband and her bodyguard. Harding later admitted to wanting Kerrigan out of the Olympics so that she could win, but she never admitted direct involvement in planning the assault. Despite the injury, Kerrigan went on to win the silver medal at the Olympic Games. Harding was sentenced to three years' probation and was banned forever from participating in skating events run by the U.S. Figure Skating Association.

The need to win in sports that Harding felt begins very early. Little League Baseball players and Pop Warner football youths often receive the same message: Be number one; win at all costs. Some coaches, even at these early levels of athletics, teach their players that they will never be truly happy or satisfied with anything less than victory.

For instance, Fred Engh, president of the National Alliance for Youth Sports, once met with a number of nine-year-old football players prior to a game. One child told him: "Coach told us that if we can put the [opposing team's] quarterback out of the game, they won't stand a chance against us."[32] Engh comments on this remark: "At the age of nine, these children were being indoctrinated into the philosophy that winning at all costs was the only thing that mattered, and that cheating and brutality were not only acceptable forms of behavior, but virtuous acts when they lead to the all-important goal of winning."[33] In fact, according to a survey done by the Minnesota Amateur Sports Commission, nearly 10 percent of players admitted they had been told or pressured to intentionally hurt another player in order to win a game.

SPORTS DOES NOT ALWAYS BUILD CHARACTER AND GOOD SPORTSMANSHIP

"A major justification for our nation's enormous investment in competitive sports is that sports build character, teach team effort, and encourage sportsmanship and fair play. Instead of learning fair play and teamwork, too many of our children are learning winning is everything."—Canadian Centres for Teaching Peace

Canadian Centres for Teaching Peace. "Sports: When Winning Is the Only Thing, Can Violence Be Far Away?" www.peace.ca/sports/htm.

Critics of such stringent messages that winning is everything contend that those children who cannot live up to the pressure of always winning may lose self-esteem. Many children, in fact, quit youth sports because of such pressure. The Canadian Centres for

Winning at All Costs: Drug Use

The winning-at-all costs attitude can produce its own set of problems. The pressure to continue winning becomes enormous. As a result, a player may often justify doing whatever is necessary to stay on top. Many such players turn to performance-enhancing drugs to help them meet this goal. Authors Lynn M. Jamieson and Thomas J. Orr explain: "The use of performance enhancing substances is common in all types of sport, and will continue to be so as long as athletes believe that the substances will actually enhance their performance. The monetary rewards available to athletes and those around them have fueled a boom in the development of both legal and illegal performance enhancing substances."

Athletes who use drugs think the drugs are actually making them stronger. These athletes believe that drugs, especially steroids, will help muscle growth and improve their strength and athletic capabilities. Professional baseball player Barry Bonds, for instance, reportedly turned to steroids when his supremacy in hitting home runs was threatened by Sammy Sosa and Mark McGwire. Other players in other sports have also turned to drugs to improve their performance on the field of play. While steroids can help build bulky muscles, they do not guarantee improved athletic ability and can lead to long-term cardiac and other medical problems.

Each professional sports league, as well as amateur sports organizations, now has its own set of rules regarding drug testing, along with different levels of punishment for first, second, and third offenses. While mandatory drug testing has been required in a number of professional and amateur sports, testing cannot always detect all illegal substances.

Lynn M. Jamieson and Thomas J. Orr. *Sport and Violence: A Critical Examination of Sport.* Burlington, MA: Butterworth-Heinemann, 2009, p. 81.

Teaching Peace reports: "Researchers have learned that when the emphasis is on winning in youth sports, most kids cease to have fun. The emphasis on winning deprives youth of the pleasure of [simply] playing the game."[34] Sportsmanship and personal development often fall by the wayside.

Some youth coaches, however, do not follow the prescription that winning is everything. There are numerous examples of coaches who teach good sportsmanship and character; they send the message that children should have fun on the athletic field. Writer Carleton Kendrick elaborates: "Coaches who equate 'trying your best' as the definition of success—and who value, expand, and demand good sportsmanship from their players—help shape the moral, ethical, and spiritual character of children."[35]

While coaches can contribute to the winning-at-all-costs attitude, other factors can also impact a young player. Some young athletes feel pressure from teammates to win and rely on violent actions to accomplish that goal. A number of young players, in their desire to win scholarships and earn a spot on college or professional teams, may also resort to violence in order to impress coaches and management.

The pressure to win continues at the collegiate and professional level as well. By that time, many players have been well indoctrinated into the winning-is-everything philosophy. Many sociologists, psychologists, and sports analysts believe that this philosophy is one of the primary causes of violence in sport. In a study that investigated perceptions of violence in sports, collegians Larry M. Lance and Charlynn E. Ross discovered that "stress on winning at any cost has brought about increased acceptance of violence as a means to achieve that end."[36]

The Warrior Athlete

The focus on winning, some experts believe, has also resulted in players who are not just athletes but warriors as well. Writers Jamieson and Orr elaborate: "The warrior athlete represents the ideals of our culture. Athletes are encouraged to embrace violence and aggression as a tool of the trade. Athletes and spectators are groomed to celebrate big hits, dangerous plays, and fights between players as a necessary part of the game. Hitting opponents and having large scale fights on the field is often accepted."[37]

A number of sports experts link the warrior athlete attitude to an exaggerated sense of masculine pride or machismo. They point out that sports aggression is almost exclusively a male behavior and suggest that any defeat in the athletic arena may be seen as a severe blow to the athlete's manhood. Author Coakley elaborates: "In many societies today, participation in power and performance sports has become an important way to prove masculinity. . . . Boys and men who play . . . sports learn quickly that they are evaluated in terms of their ability to do violence in combination with physical skills."[38] As a result, violence is thought to be one way to protect one's pride and masculinity.

SPORTS CAN BUILD SPORTSMANSHIP

"Sports participation . . . develops a positive self-image; teaches [children] how to work as a team; . . . teaches how to respect others."—American Sport Education Program

Quoted in Dawn Ramsburg. "Children and Sports: Don't Forget to Practice Sportsmanship." KidSource. www.kidsource.com/kidsource/content4/children.sports.pn.html.

The media help perpetuate the concept of the sports star as a warrior. The parallels between sports and war are constantly reiterated with reference to words such as battling, blitz, trenches, attack, sacked, and others. Coakley explains: "Professional athletes are entertainers, and they [sports management] now use a promotional and heroic rhetoric that presents images of revenge, retaliation, hate, hostility, intimidation, aggression, violence, domination, and destruction."[39]

Author George Orwell perhaps summed up the concept of sports as war best when he wrote: "Serious sport has nothing to do with fair play. It is bound up with hatred, jealousy, boastfulness, disregard of all rules, and sadistic pleasure in witnessing violence; in other words, it is war without the shooting."[40]

Demands by Fans and Management

In part, the image of the warrior athlete is valuable because it is supported and idolized by sports fans and management. The National Football League (NFL), the National Hockey League (NHL), and the National Basketball Association (NBA), for instance, all use these kinds of images to promote their games. Advertisements for upcoming big sporting events, for instance, such as ice hockey's Stanley Cup Final and the Super Bowl in professional football, frequently contain footage of violent hits.

Marketers contend that such images attract larger audiences. Coakley summarizes: "Their marketing people know that violence and moral outrage about violence attracts audiences and generates profits."[41] Whether it is the footage that is shown or simply the interest generated by championships that accounts for the audience is a matter of debate among sociologists.

Profit is a big motivation in professional sports. Television contracts run in the millions of dollars. Thus, the difference between a good season and a losing season can translate into large amounts of money for all involved. Because of this, players are encouraged to use any tactic, including violence, to help their team win and generate more profit through fan interest and ticket sales. Sellouts and packed stadiums are the rule for teams that win consistently. Winning teams also appear more often on television than teams that frequently lose.

A team's fans can also increase the tendency toward violence. A case in point is National Association for Stock Car Racing

Upcoming sporting events are often promoted by the media with footage that includes violent hits and bench-clearing brawls.

(NASCAR). It is generally believed by sports analysts and behavioral experts that many people attend or participate in stock car races specifically because of the potential for violence. Many spectators, in fact, confess that they come because of the prospect of witnessing spectacular accidents. When that does not happen, the fans stay away. NASCAR driver Greg Biffle further explains:

> We've lost fans . . . there's a percentage of fans that want to see a crash. A wreck. . . . These new cars don't crash as much as we used to. The old car, we had crashes. Now people don't spin out. . . . For whatever percentage of fans who want to see that wreck and see that car in smoke and sparks and stuff flying, those fans are not satisfied anymore. And no matter what we do, we're not going to satisfy those fans unless we crash. And none of us want to crash.[42]

In a similar fashion, ice hockey fans often attend games because of the potential for violence. A'Don Allen, sports director for a news channel in Elmira, New York, agrees: "The entire arena erupts with cheering when there are fights," said Allen. "Even if their team is losing, the fans still get excited when they see two players pummeling each other."[43]

Sports Rage: Revenge and Retaliation

With violence being approved and even encouraged by fans and management, it is not unusual for the violence on the field to get

Sports analysts and behavioral experts generally believe that many people attend NASCAR races specifically because of the potential for violence and car wrecks.

out of control. With players focused on winning, rage, usually taking the form of violent retaliation, is sometimes the result. A player or team, for instance, may decide to retaliate against another player or team when they feel that a violent act was not penalized or punished. Retaliation is essentially returning a like action—hurting someone who hurt you.

THERE IS MORE TO SPORTS THAN WINNING

"You win not only because you win games but because you build character in the athletes you coach."—Positive Coaching Alliance

Quoted in Lynn M. Jamieson and Thomas J. Orr. *Sport and Violence: A Critical Examination of Sport.* Burlington, MA: Butterworth-Heinmann, 2009, p. 169.

Players from several different sports engage in acts of retaliation and consider them a normal part of the sport. In baseball, for instance, a pitcher sometimes purposely hits a batter with the baseball in order to rectify an earlier act of violence committed by an opposing pitcher. Journalist Sergio Bonilla explains: "'You hit one of ours; well, we will hit one of yours.' That is the basic premise behind pitcher retaliation in baseball. It is one of those traditions that has been around since the game started."[44] Sometimes the pitcher decides on this move; other times it is the manager who calls for a pitch aimed at the batter's head. This practice is extremely prevalent in Major League Baseball, as well as at other levels of baseball. While it is often difficult to determine whether a pitch thrown at a player's head is intentional or not, baseball's record book lists dozens of pitchers who have been labeled as "headhunters" for their history of deliberately throwing at other players. And in a recent example of a coach ordering such a throw, the head varsity coach of Allegheny-Limestone High School in New York was suspended indefinitely in May 2010 for ordering one of his pitchers to throw at an opposing player.

This kind of retaliation can be very dangerous. Pitchers control a very hard ball that can be thrown at speeds in excess of

100 miles per hour (161kph). The potential for serious injury increases dramatically when the ball connects with a batter's head. The record books are filled with players' names who have been injured. In 1920 Cleveland Indian batter Ray Chapman, for example, was hit in the head by a pitch thrown by Carl Mays of the New York Yankees. Chapman's head was split open, and he died some fourteen hours later.

Acts of revenge and retaliation also occur all too frequently in ice hockey; often with tragic consequences. On February 16, 2004, for instance, Steve Moore, a player with the Colorado Avalanche, injured Vancouver Canucks team captain Markus Näslund by knocking him in the head with his elbow. No penalty was called on the play, despite Näslund's suffering a concussion and subsequently missing three games. While the hit drew criticism from the Canucks players, the NHL ruled that the hit was legal.

Vancouver players, however, would not let the matter rest, and swore they would get revenge against Moore in a future game. Canucks general manager Brad May urged his team to exact revenge; he stated: "There's definitely a bounty on his head. . . . It's going to be fun when we get him."[45] The retaliation came in a game on March 8, 2004. Canucks player Todd Bertuzzi, with a reputation for violent hits, was sent on the ice late in the third period. After failing to get Moore to fight with him, Bertuzzi skated after him and punched Moore in the head from behind and then fell on him, along with several other players from both teams. Moore's head was driven into the ice, causing three fractured neck vertebrae, facial cuts, and a concussion. He lay on the ice, motionless and unconscious for over ten minutes. Moore suffered a broken neck and a concussion; he never played hockey again. Bertuzzi was immediately suspended for the remainder of the season and had to reapply for reinstatement the next season. Moore later commented on the hit: "I think that type of (retribution) stuff doesn't have any place in the game."[46]

Another act of retaliation occurred during a professional soccer match. Roy Keane of Manchester United seriously injured another player who had hit him three years earlier. Keane slid forcefully into the other player's knee, actually tackling him, in

In Major League Baseball if a ball is thrown at a player, his team typically retaliates by hitting a player on the opposing team.

a very violent and intentional move. Keane was ejected from the game; the other player never recovered from the injury and was forced to retire from soccer. According to writer Kerr, Keane later admitted in his autobiography "that he deliberately set out to injure [the other player] in the match in a premeditated act of revenge. . . . When asked if he had any regrets, Keane replied: 'No . . . I had no remorse. . . . He got his just rewards.'"[47]

A number of retaliatory incidents have also occurred in stock car racing. Drivers often bump other cars with the intent of forcing another driver out of the race. In a 1986 race in Asheville, North Carolina, for example, driver Jack Ingram was battling for the lead when he tangled with two other cars and was forced off the track. In an attempt to get even, he turned around and drove straight into one of the other cars, injuring the driver so badly that he had to be hospitalized.

With violent retaliation occurring in a number of sports, most sociologists and sports psychologists agree that the leagues must take steps to prevent further incidents. With such a high premium on winning and aggressive play, however, sports rage and retaliation may be difficult issues to address.

Are Sports Teaching Sportsmanship?

With such an emphasis on winning and with an increased prevalence of violence in sports, many sports experts have begun to question where sportsmanship fits into the sport equation. Sportsmanship is generally defined as a standard of conduct in which athletes pursue victory in a courteous and fair way. Sports can provide an exceptional setting for learning and character development. Most experts agree that this must begin at the youth level of sports.

WINNING IS EVERYTHING

"If winning isn't everything, why do they keep score?"—Vince Lombardi, former coach of the Green Bay Packers

Quoted in Quote Garden. "Quotations About Sports." www.quotegarden.com/sports .html.

Some of the primary responsibility for teaching sportsmanship falls on the coach. Writers Christine Nucci and Young-Shim Kim contend: "Unsportsmanlike behaviors of young athletes are learned and reinforced depending upon the type of sport and leadership of coaches. . . . Sport participation facilitates and teaches sportsmanship and moral reasoning if quality leaderships and environments are provided."[48] While coaches are often considered responsible for dictating how a player approaches his or her sport, the qualities of sportsmanship can also be learned from a player's peers or other adults in his or her life, such as parents, siblings, and friends.

The Josephson Institute, a group dedicated to improving the ethical quality of society, believes that there are six essential elements of character building and sportsmanship that sports

The Ultimate in Sports Rage—Terrorism

Acts of terrorism are the ultimate forms of violence and sports rage. Authors Lynn M. Jamieson and Thomas J. Orr explain: "The power of the World Olympics . . . may not be the perfect place for a crowd riot, but the same visibility and connection to culture issues and ideas of a population can be a powerful way to shock a national consciousness. The Munich shootings, bombings in Atlanta's summer games, and the constant threats at American sporting events have been sad reminders of the connection between sports, power, and cultural rage."[1]

Several sporting events have brought acts of terrorism into the public eye. The first was the Munich, Germany, massacre. On September 3, 1972, the Israeli team at the Olympic Games was attacked by a group of Palestinian terrorists. Ten athletes were killed, along with one coach, members of the terrorist group, and police officers. Security has been much stronger at Olympic events since that violence. Bill Payne, who was in charge of security at the 1996 Atlanta games, stated: "You hire the best experts, you spend incredible amounts of time and money and you hope you've covered all contingencies."[2] Even the best security in Atlanta, however, did not deter a terrorist from planting a bomb that went off and killed one spectator.

Since the terrorist attacks of September 11, 2001, planners of sporting events have become even more security conscious. The high visibility of large and important sporting events along with the large quantities of people who attend them make such events prime terrorist targets. Patrons at sporting events today must go through metal detectors as well as visual checks by arena officials. Purses are searched, and backpacks and other carriers are forbidden.

1. Lynn M. Jamieson and Thomas J. Orr. *Sport and Violence: A Critical Examination of Sport*. Burlington, MA: Butterworth-Heinemann, 2009, p. 55.
2. Quoted in Tim Dahlberg. "Olympics No Stranger to Threats of Violence." *Albany (NY) Times Union*, September 13, 2001.

The first sporting event to bring an act of terrorism into the public eye was the 1972 Munich Olympics massacre. Here, officials negotiate with one of the Munich terrorists.

can embody: trustworthiness, respect, responsibility, fairness, caring, and citizenship. Trustworthiness involves never cheating and honoring the rules of the sport. An athlete that has respect can win or lose with class, while showing appreciation of their opponent and respecting the calls made by officials. Responsibility includes maintaining safe conditions on the playing field and being a role model for other players and younger people. Playing by the rules and treating everyone properly are evidence of fairness; while ensuring the safety and welfare of other athletes encompasses caring. Finally, being a good citizen includes playing by the rules and upholding the principles of sportsmanship.

Sportsmanship can often go by the wayside when a team's emphasis is all about winning. The president of the National Alliance for Youth Sports, Fred Engh, elaborates: "During the last couple of decades, professional, collegiate, and even high school sports have undergone a remarkable transformation. Sportsmanship and fair play have become virtually nonexistent, while incidents of cheating, taunting, attacking officials, and running up the score [playing aggressively when winning is already guaranteed] have increased dramatically."[49] These attitudes have also trickled down into youth athletics.

Kerr further elaborates on sportsmanship in youth sports:

> It is interesting that, unlike adults, young athletes often show a concern for their opponents. However, this sympathy for others, it seems, does not take long to disappear. The same kind of attitude from sport education that drives young athletes and teams to focus on defeating opponents, also encourages them to think of their participation in sport purely from their own point of view. Opponents are disparaged and some coaches even try to foster in their athletes an active dislike for other competitors.[50]

An overemphasis on winning can lead both to issues of sportsmanship and the concept of sports as a war that must be won at all costs. This emphasis often leads to overly aggressive players who commit acts of sports rage. It can also lead to violence off the field of play.

THE SPILLOVER OF SPORTS VIOLENCE: OFF-THE-FIELD VIOLENCE

Journalist Mike Imren asserts: "Violence by athletes has become epidemic."[51] He was referring not to on-the-field violence but to the acts of off-the-field violence perpetrated by athletes from nearly every major sport.

Most sports analysts claim that it is very difficult to make the transition from a violent playing field to a nonviolent life off the field. Jessie Armstead, a linebacker in the National Football League (NFL), for example, stated: "During a game we want to kill each other. Then we're told to shake hands and drive home safely."[52] John Niland, a former football player, agrees: "Any athlete who thinks he can be as violent as you can be playing football and leave it all on the field, is kidding himself."[53]

In fact, in a survey done by researchers Jeff Benedict and Don Yaeger, it was found that one in five NFL players surveyed during the 1996–1997 season had been charged with some kind of serious criminal act. In 1997 alone, thirty-eight players in the NFL were arrested for violent crimes. The analysts also collected data on NBA players during the 2001–2002 season and discovered that 40 percent of them had a police record involving a serious crime.

It is not just professional athletes who are involved in off-the-field violence. Researchers have also discovered that university athletes are more likely than other students to be accused of rape, assault, break-ins, and drug trafficking. Derek A. Kreager is an assistant professor of sociology in the Crime, Law, and Justice program at Penn State University. In the late 1990s, using a

Compared with nonathletes, football and wrestling athletes are 40 percent more likely to get into a serious fight.

national database of over six thousand students from 120 different schools, Kreager analyzed the effects of team sports on male interpersonal violence. He concluded: "Compared with nonathletes, football players and wrestlers faced higher risks of getting into a serious fight by more than 40%. High contact sports that are associated with aggression and masculinity increase the risk of violence. Players are encouraged to be violent outside the sport because they are rewarded for being violent inside it."[54]

Sportswriter John Feinstein summarizes the problem of off-the-field violence: "There is no question that there is a problem in a sport where you are told all week to work yourself into a fever pitch to go out and commit violence and then told, once you're off the field, that that's not part of your life. Most athletes can separate the two, but some of them clearly can't."[55]

Athletes and Guns

Much of the violence that occurs off the field involves guns and gun crime. Guns have increasingly become part of the culture of American sports. Newspaper journalist Greg Couch of the *Chicago Sun Times* elaborates: "Sports and guns have an uneasy but growing connection. . . . Athletes apparently are becoming more and more well-armed, as part of a trend, and that often is leading to trouble."[56] Former NFL player Lomas Brown, for instance, told the *New York Times* that guns are common in the NFL: "Just about every guy I played with in the NFL had a gun. Guns are rampant in football. . . . It's a disaster waiting to happen."[57]

Richard Lapchick of the Center for the Study of Sport in Society and other sports analysts disagree. Lapchick and others contend that an athlete's use of guns is just more publicized than that of "ordinary" citizens. Lapchick, for instance, according to Couch, "cites numbers saying that firearms are in 39% of American homes. And we don't know how many athletes have guns."[58]

ATHLETES NO MORE LIKELY TO COMMIT OFF-THE-FIELD VIOLENCE

"It's unfair to criticize athletes without examining American culture, which has become more violent in general. Statistically, a pro basketball or football player is no more likely to be involved in violent behavior, either as a perpetrator or a victim, than anyone else."—Richard Lapchick, founder of Northeastern University's Center for the Study of Sport in Society

Quoted in Joseph Williams. "Packed with Trouble: Mix of Athletes, Guns Is Problem." *Boston Globe*, December 23, 2008.

Today professional sports leagues are attempting to address the gun issue by having a clear-cut gun policy for all players. These policies state that guns in any form are dangerous. Furthermore, players are forbidden to have weapons in the locker room, on the team plane, or on any football property. Players are also cautioned not to carry guns in any situation that might bring them danger. Carrying a gun, even for reasons of self-defense, can often lead to trouble. Journalist Joseph Williams of the *Boston Globe* explains: "Athletes, particularly African-Americans, have become targets for criminals, leading some of them to arm themselves, increasing the possibility that something bad will happen to them or someone else."[59]

New York Giants football star Plaxico Burress was one player who ignored the gun policy and other recommendations of the NFL. Burress, in a period of one year, went from being a Super

Bowl hero to a prison inmate. He accidently shot himself in the leg with an unlicensed gun in a New York City nightclub in November 2008. He was charged with a violation of the gun laws and was sentenced to two years in prison. As a result, he missed two seasons of football during the peak years of his career. At the time of his release, Burress was thirty-four years old; possibly too old to resume his career.

Gilbert Arenas, one of the rising stars in professional basketball, is another player who got in trouble for carrying guns. He was charged with bringing several unloaded guns into the Washington Wizards locker room in December 2009. One of the Wizards' best players, Arenas pleaded guilty. "I now recognize that what I did was a mistake and was wrong," Arenas stated. "And I now realize that there is no such thing as joking around when it comes to a gun—even if unloaded."[60]

New York Giants football star Plaxico Burress leaves court after pleading guilty to violating gun laws. He was sentenced to two years in prison.

Crimes Against Women

While gun violence is far too common among athletes, violent crimes against women also account for a major portion of off-the-field incidents. Professional athletes commit their own share of such crimes, but the statistics for crimes such as rape and sexual assault have reached alarming rates on college campuses. Author and teacher Jeff Benedict made the first national study of sexual assault and athletes in the 1990s. He discovered that male athletes make up about 3.3 percent of collegiate populations, yet they represent 19 percent of sexual assault perpetrators.

CONTACT SPORTS AND OFF-FIELD VIOLENCE LINKED

"A study by researchers at Penn State University . . . suggests that athletes who participate in contact-heavy team sports, such as football, are more likely to commit violence off the field."
—Taylor de Lench, journalist and author of "Contact Sports and off-the-Field Violence Linked, Study Says"

Taylor de Lench. "Contact Sports and off-the-Field Violence Linked, Study Says." MomsTeam. www.momsteam.com/successful-parenting/youth-sports-parenting-basics/parenting-boys/contact-sports-linked-to-off-the-f.

A number of different writers have addressed the question about why athletes commit such crimes. Journalist Mike Imrem, for instance, questions whether the physical and often violent nature of an athlete's training is responsible. He elaborates: "Does the nature of their training translate into abusing women? Athletes are conditioned to be physical, to increase their power, to be aggressive, to be unyielding, to confront challenges, to defy opposition, most of all to win, win, win."[61] With such an emphasis on a male athlete's power and performance, playing sports can often promote the image of women as someone to be pursued and conquered.

Female victims of sexual violence on campus, however, sometimes find their claims are challenged and their attackers escape punishment of any kind. ABC reporter Connie Chung elaborates: "Violence against women is a serious problem on college campuses, and victims who come forward sometimes find themselves fighting the school as well as their attacker."[62]

In an effort to explain why university officials often fail to punish offenders, Andrew SkinnerLopata, an attorney who defends victims of violence, examined the issue in March 2010. SkinnerLopata wrote about an outbreak of violence on the University of Oregon campus, during which six football players were charged with various crimes of violence against women. According to SkinnerLopata, the response by head coach Chip Kelly and Oregon's athletic director was minimal. SkinnerLopata explains: "If a player is a vital part of the team and is charged with a violent crime against a woman, there will be no rush to judgment and the player will face no disciplinary action."[63]

What happened to two women in 1994 is yet another example of the mentality that prevails on some college campuses. Kathy Redmond was allegedly raped by a University of Nebraska football star and reported the incident to police as well as to the university. Redmond, in an interview with Chung, reported that she had real misgivings that anything would be done:

> [The victim] gets a real feeling of isolation because they think the fans and coaches and management feel that it's a personal attack against them . . . so when you level a charge against an athlete, then all of a sudden you're not battling the athlete, you're battling a whole mindset, you're battling fans, you're battling coaches, you're battling sports management.[64]

Redmond eventually sued the university and received a cash award; the coach also later apologized. The player was never disciplined or charged with a crime.

Christy Brzonkala was also allegedly raped; she was assaulted by a group of football players from Virginia Tech University. She went to the Virginia Tech coach and reported the rape. The coach's response is indicative of the attitude found at some universities: "You know, I'm sorry this happened, but we need to protect our players."[65] The only punishment handed out was that one of the perpetrators had to attend a one-hour

Kathy Redmond, allegedly raped by a University of Nebraska football player, went on to found the National Coalition Against Violent Athletes.

educational session. There were no criminal charges filed; no suspensions from the team.

SkinnerLopata believes that this failure to punish athletes for such crimes sends the wrong kind of message. He writes that athletes receive the following message: "First, that the athletes and the team are all that matters. . . . Second, that male violence against women is acceptable. Third, the bigger star you are, the more you can get away with. Finally, that the athletes really make the rules and that the coaches just try to do damage control. Essentially the message is . . . 'boys will be boys.'"[66]

Sportswriter John Feinstein agrees; he contends that because athletes are often put on pedestals in modern society, the assumption is that the players are thus above the law. "They are given special privileges in terms of when they go to class,"

"Ghetto Loyalty"

Many athletes struggle when they enter the world of professional sports. Many of these young men are ill prepared for the stardom they find and the responsibilities that come with that stardom.

Athletes, especially those who come from poverty-stricken neighborhoods, may have difficulty separating themselves from their background. They often surround themselves with childhood friends, some of whom may even have criminal records. This is called "ghetto loyalty" and arises from a sense of indebtedness. Jonathan Chaney, a former gang member in California, explains: "A lot of time if you grew up in a gang-infested area and you are a good athlete, you will get a pass on participating in criminal activity. . . . That comes with a price. Once famous, the former friends come back and say . . . 'you owe us.'"[1] This is often to the detriment of the athlete. Rather than rely on the mentors provided by the professional teams, the athletes rely instead on their childhood friends, who may often provide bad advice.

Part of the problem also derives from the fact that stardom brings money, big homes, jewelry, and fancy cars. This is a huge leap for someone who grew up in poverty. Many athletes are not prepared to deal with their fame. David Cornwell, an Atlanta lawyer who represents star athletes, explains: "Sometimes the cultural influences athletes face aren't being offset by their advisers, their team, the league they play in."[2]

To help these athletes make the adjustment, the National Football League, for instance, now has different programs that offer guidance for all new players on the best way to acclimate to the responsibilities of stardom. One of the topics covered is that of ghetto loyalty.

1. Quoted in George Dohrmann and Farrell Evans. "The Road to Bad Newz." *Sports Illustrated*, November 27, 2007, p. 74.
2. Quoted in Dorhrmann and Evans. "The Road to Bad Newz, p. 72"

Feinstein writes, "and in terms of the meals they eat, in terms of the way they live their lives day in and day out, and they come to believe, to some degree, some of them, that they're above the law in all cases and all situations because they're forgiven their mistakes."[67] Many experts in the field of sports violence believe that this sense of being above the law, and thus entitled, begins early in a player's life, sometimes as early as high school.

Entitlement

Some star athletes believe that they are not subject to the rules that govern others. This comes from a sense of entitlement that derives in part from a long record of leniency toward sports stars in the United States and elsewhere. *Christian Science Monitor* editors contend: "The attitude begins early, allowing high school and college players to escape responsibility for violent behavior. . . . [In addition,] some sociologists say the feeling of invincibility that comes with multimillion dollar National Football League contracts doesn't help to check bad behavior."[68] This is true in other sports leagues as well.

Most athletes are perceived as heroes by the general public. Their stardom and hero status seem to protect these athletes from official reprimands and punishment. Because the athletes are viewed by the community with awe and fascination, sometimes fans, sports administrators, and officials are willing to overlook actions that might otherwise be condemned. Melvin C. Ray, assistant professor of sociology at Mississippi State University, elaborates: "Athletes are put on a pedestal. They are given almost free rein to do what they want as long as their teams are in the Top 20."[69]

Professional golfer Tiger Woods explains how this sense of being entitled led to his own fall from grace. After admitting to having a number of illicit sexual relationships outside his marriage, he explained:

> I was unfaithful. I had affairs. I cheated. What I did is not acceptable, and I am the only person to blame. I stopped living by the core values I was taught to believe in. I knew my actions were wrong, but I convinced myself that normal rules didn't apply. Instead I thought only about myself. . . . I thought I could get away with whatever I wanted to. I felt that I . . . deserved to enjoy all the temptations around me. I felt that I was entitled. . . . I was wrong. I don't get to play by different rules.[70]

Athletes as Victims of Violence

This sense of feeling entitled to preferential treatment, however, has a dark side. In addition to sometimes being the perpetrators of violent crime, athletes are also frequently the victims of such crimes. Athletes are all too often not only being threatened but killed. Many popular athletes, for instance, receive death threats; it is another part of the price they pay for fame.

ATHLETES SHOULD NOT BE ABLE TO CONTINUE SPORTS ONCE CONVICTED

"A survey reveals: 76% of United States adults and 82% of teens think that it is bad for society to allow athletes to continue their sports career when convicted of a serious crime."—Bethany P. Withers, Harvard Law School student

Bethany P. Withers. "The Integrity of the Game: Professional Athletes and Domestic Violence." *Journal of Sports and Entertainment Law*, April 2010. http://harvardjsel.com/wp-content/uploads/2010/04/JSEL-Withers.pdf.

One of the most famous death threats in sports occurred in a sport not known for its violence: golf. During the 1977 U.S. Open, golfer Hubert Green "had to withstand not only a final-round challenge from his rivals but also a death threat over the last four holes,"[71] reports *Sports Illustrated* journalist Dan Jenkins.

Green had only four holes to play when he was approached by a golf official and informed that a telephone call had been received by the FBI. The female caller said that three of her friends were going to kill Green. Despite the threat, Green opted to continue play, with police in surveillance along the way. Police officers in pith helmets and riot gear, along with detectives in golf clothes, kept a close eye on the crowds that lined the fairways. The television network provided some of their cameras to help look for threats. After sinking the final and winning putt, Green was hurried into the clubhouse, where he was surrounded by golf officials and police officers. No armed suspects were found; no arrests were ever made.

Hundreds of other athletes have received similar threats over the years. Journalist Mark Reason elaborates: "Death threats are now a part of sport and society."[72] In May 2009, for instance, ice hockey superstar Alexander Ovechkin of the Washington Capitals was threatened by a fan who wrote in an e-mail: "I'm killing Ovechkin. I'll go to jail. I don't care."[73] Prior to breaking Hank Aaron's home run record, baseball star Barry Bonds received death threats, as did Hank Aaron when he closed in on Babe Ruth's record. Professional sports do not have the monopoly on such threats. In June 2009 former University of Tennessee quarterback Jonathan Crompton acknowledged that he had received death threats. Denver Nuggets professional basketball player Kenyon Martin says: "It's just the nature of things now. You're not safe nowhere. . . . We're targets."[74]

Denver Broncos cornerback Darrent Williams was killed in a drive-by shooting in Denver in 2007.

Sometimes, instead of just receiving death threats, athletes are actually attacked and killed. Darrent Williams, a Denver Broncos football player, for instance, was shot and killed when someone opened fire on his automobile in 2007. His death is believed to be the result of a fight between gang members and several members of Williams's entourage. Also in 2007, another football player, Sean Taylor of the Washington Redskins, was killed in his home by burglars in Florida. Taylor apparently was targeted because of his wealth by four young men, two of whom had loose ties to the player. In 2008 Richard Collier, a lineman with the Jacksonville Jaguars, was paralyzed when assailants shot him fourteen times as he headed home after a night out.

Hazing

One form of off-the-field violence has been garnering increased media attention in today's society. This kind of violence is called hazing and includes, according to writers Lynn M. Jamieson and Thomas J. Orr, "any activity expected of someone joining a group that humiliates, degrades, abuses, or endangers, regardless of the person's willingness to participate." High school, college, and even professional sports teams often include such initiation ceremonies as a rite of passage.

Cases of hazing are being documented at alarming rates. Many such ceremonies involve alcohol-related initiations, and over two-thirds of the people being hazed are subjected to humiliation rituals. Athletes can be subjected to such rituals as drinking alcohol until they vomit or pass out, being hit or punched with an object, or being forced to submit to sexual acts. Nearly all hazing inflicts physical or mental harm to those being initiated.

Hazing is very common from the middle school level through the university level. According to research done by analyst K. Bushweller in 2000, 80 percent of college athletes have experienced hazing, along with 40 percent of high school athletes and one out of every twenty middle school athletes. These numbers, claim sociologists, are probably low; many athletes fail to report incidents because of embarrassment and the fear of possible repercussions.

Lynn M. Jamieson and Thomas J. Orr. *Sport and Violence: A Critical Examination of Sport.* Burlington, MA: Butterworth-Heinemann, 2009, p. 171.

There are a number of theories as to why these players become victims of violence. Overzealous fans can often become violent when their favorite players do not win, while jealous friends and foes sometimes strike back against what they view as the rich superstars who ignore them. Criminals also know that these athletes often keep many valuables in their homes and on their persons. Writer Samuel Bell Jr. elaborates: "The rich nature of athletics, particularly the NBA and NFL, make the athletes . . . targets for impoverished, unruly criminals who look to take what they can from them."[75]

ATHLETES SHOULD BE GIVEN A SECOND CHANCE

"I'm proud we were the team that gave him a second chance. I think the country is really built around this. It's an important principle. Because he served his time."—Jeffrey Lurie, owner of the Philadelphia Eagles of the National Football League, upon signing Michael Vick following Vick's release from prison after serving a sentence on dogfighting charges

Quoted in S.L. Price. "Is It OK to Cheer?" *Sports Illustrated*, November 29, 2010, p. 38.

The proliferation of off-the-field violence is a continuing problem in sports. So too are the acts of violence perpetrated by nonathletes, such as spectators, parents, and coaches.

CHAPTER 4

VIOLENCE BY NONATHLETES: SPECTATORS, COACHES, AND PARENTS

The athletes who commit violent acts on and off the field are not the only people involved in sports violence. Spectator violence, for instance, has become a significant problem in many sports. Fans have been known to engage in violent acts against athletes, other fans, coaches, and referees. In numerous incidents, spectator violence has also escalated into riots in the stands and around athletic arenas. Parents of young athletes have also committed many acts of violence, as have coaches at all levels of athletic endeavor.

Hooliganism

One of the most extreme forms of spectator violence has been occurring with increasing frequency since the early 1960s in Europe. Called hooliganism, this form of spectator violence is common to international soccer matches. The term *hooliganism* was first used by English security forces to describe the violence that was happening in soccer games in that country. Writer Rit Nosotro elaborates: "In Europe, fans of the winning team would walk around chanting ceaselessly, 'we're number one!' Then they might set fires or overturn things from garbage cans to cars."[76]

Soccer is unique in sports today in that it is the only sport where violence among spectators is often worse than among players. International soccer attracts tremendous crowds around the world; it is not unusual for as many as two hundred thousand people to attend big soccer matches. Soccer fans take their teams and the games very seriously, and the threat of violence is always present. Writers Lynn M. Jamieson and Thomas J. Orr explain: "Hooligans often travel to the opposing teams' city to vandalize their opponents' town. The Hooligans representing each team . . . square off and fight their battles . . . What started as a battle of fists sometimes has become a battle of weapons. . . . Many times the police who attempted to stop the fighting or vandalism was victimized and even killed."[77]

Fights between soccer fans of opposing sides often occur because the fans develop a close personal bond with their towns' teams.

The reason for hooliganism has been partially explained by the fact that soccer teams in Great Britain and other European countries are community based. This can lead to intense rivalries between towns and their teams. As a community develops strong emotional bonds with its soccer team, the town often takes losses as personal defeats. This leads to great tension between communities that sometimes bubbles over in riots and other violence at soccer games between the two teams. Violence can occur not only during and after a soccer match but also prior to a game. Fights often erupt in bars and neighborhoods the night before a big match.

INDIVIDUALS LOSE FOCUS IN CROWDS

"They [individual fans] no longer think as individuals. No one feels personally responsible as long as he or she is doing what everyone else is doing."—Delia S. Saenz, a psychology professor at the University of Notre Dame

Quoted in Charles Leersheen. "When Push Comes to Shove." *Newsweek*, May 16, 1988, p. 16.

Fights and other violence can also lead to death; death statistics as a result of hooliganism are staggering. In April 1989, for example, 95 fans were killed and over 100 were injured when spectators pushed and shoved their way into a soccer game in Sheffield, England. A few years later, in 1995, 39 were killed and over 400 injured in a riot that occurred at a match between Great Britain and an Italian team in Belgium. Soccer riots, in particular, have resulted in hundreds of deaths around the world.

The violent actions of English soccer fans in the 1980s, for instance, caused English teams to be banned from European competition for an indefinite period of time following what came to be known as the Heysel Stadium disaster in 1985. In the finals of the European Cup tournament, a masonry wall collapsed under the weight of rioting fans in Heysel Stadium in Brussels, Belgium. Forty-one fans were killed; another 150 injured. Twenty-seven rioters were arrested, with a number of Liverpool fans prosecuted for manslaughter for their role in the riot. The ban on English teams playing on the continent of Europe was finally lifted for the 1990–1991 season.

Hooliganism has also been responsible for a number of notorious off-the-field murders. During the 1994 World Cup soccer matches, for example, Colombian player Andres Escobar accidently kicked the ball into his own net. Afterward, on his return to Colombia, he was confronted outside a bar by a gunman who shot the player six times, killing him. Several other Colombian soccer players have met a similar fate; killed after making errors on the soccer field.

Spectator Violence

Spectator violence also occurs in sports other than soccer. Some spectators like nothing better than to see violent acts on the field of play in many sports. At times, they also become violent themselves. This is true in nearly every sport that is played around the world. Spectator violence can take many forms: celebratory riots, property destruction, fights among opposing fans, throwing objects on the field of play, violent confrontations with players and officials, and drunken brawls. Professor of sports psychology D. Stanley Eitzen of Colorado State University elaborates: "Sports has a dark side. . . . Spectator behavior such as rioting and throwing objects at players and officials is excessive. . . . Spectators not only tolerate violence, they sometimes encourage it."[78]

This violence is not just a modern behavior. Writers Robert M. Gorman and David Weeks explain: "As long as there have been spectator sports—even as far back as ancient Rome—there has been violence, and sometimes death, in the stands."[79] In 1900, for example, baseball umpire Phil Power was forced to carry a loaded revolver to protect himself from angry fans. Serious violence among spectators was definitely a problem during the early years of baseball. A journalist described what happened at a baseball game in 1900: "Thousands of gun-slinging Chicago Cubs fans turned a Fourth of July doubleheader into a shoot-out . . . endangering the lives of players and fellow spectators. Bullets

The Rocket Richard Riot

One of the worst incidents of spectator violence erupted in 1955 when ice hockey superstar Maurice "Rocket" Richard of the Montreal Canadiens was suspended following an incident on the ice. In addition to slashing an opponent, he also inadvertently punched an official. Richard was ejected from the game and suspended for the upcoming Stanley Cup playoffs by National Hockey League Commissioner Clarence Campbell. Montreal fans were furious.

Fans had gathered outside the arena before Campbell's arrival the evening following his decision. They spewed epithets and waved placards. Later, during the game, a fan punched Campbell in the jaw; he was also pelted with programs, eggs, shoes, and other items. During one of the intermissions, a smoke bomb exploded inside the arena and a gunshot was heard. Rushing to restore order, police used tear gas and evacuated the arena. In the panic that followed, thousands of fans stampeded into the Montreal streets, where they overturned and burned cars, looted stores, tore down trolley lines, and fought with police for seven hours. Journalist Chris Cook reports: "A rifle shot shattered a window at the [Montreal] Forum; this incited the mob to a newsstand-burning, store-looting, stone-throwing rampage that caused over $1 million damage." More than sixty people were arrested.

Chris Cook. "The Rocket Richard Riot." Suite101. www .suite101.com/content/the-rocket-richard-riot-a47582.

Montreal Canadiens fans attack National Hockey League president Clarence Campbell, right, over Campbell's decision to suspend Maurice "Rocket" Richard for punching an official in 1955.

sang, darted, and whizzed over players' heads as the rambunctious fans fired round after round whenever the Cubs scored."[80]

The sports world has witnessed thousands of incidents in the last hundred years that involved fan violence. In baseball, one of the worst happened in Cleveland, Ohio, in 1974. In the "beer night brawl," hundreds of Cleveland Indians baseball fans rushed the field and started beating up the opposing Texas Rangers players during the ninth inning of the game. Several players and one umpire were injured in the ensuing brawl. In another ugly incident, Houston Astros baseball player Bob Watson crashed into the outfield wall in Cincinnati while trying to catch a ball. As he lay unconscious and bloody on the field, his glasses shattered against his face, Cincinnati fans leaned over the stands and poured beer and ice cubes on the player and those who had come to his assistance.

Baseball is not the only sport where spectator violence is common. The biggest eruption of fan violence in boxing, for instance, occurred on July 4, 1910, after the first black heavyweight champion, Jack Johnson, had beaten the so-called White Hope, Jim Jeffries. Racial violence erupted all over the United States following the fight. U.S. Marines had to be called to Norfolk, Virginia, to restore order, while in Keystone, West Virginia, a group of armed blacks took over the town. In the days after the fight, 19 people died as a result of violence, and more than 250 were injured. Over five thousand people were arrested.

Professional football games can also turn ugly when fans get upset. A reporter for the *Cincinnati Post* gives an example of a December 2001 incident: "Standing near midfield, players and officials watched as enraged [Cleveland] Browns fans rained plastic beer bottles, cups, and debris down on them."[81] Members of the opposing team, the Jacksonville Jaguars, ran; one Jaguar player reported that it was like dodging bullets. The game was stopped for thirty minutes with forty-eight seconds left in the game. Thousands of bottles were later collected from the playing field.

Violence among spectators is also common in collegiate athletics, where some of the most destructive crowd behavior occurs during victory celebrations. After Minnesota won the collegiate hockey championship in 2002, for instance, violence broke out; seven University of Minnesota students were arrested after police sent one hundred police officers and twenty-five firefighters to restore order and put out fires. A similar incident occurred in 2002 after Ohio State defeated its archrival the University of Michigan to advance to the championship game. Fans in downtown Columbus rioted; cars were overturned and burned. Police in riot gear used tear gas to disperse the crowd.

In general, fans at noncontact sports behave better than those who attend contact sporting events, but this is not always the case. In 1993 tennis player Monica Seles was attacked by a spectator and stabbed in the back with a knife. The spectator, Günter Parche, was convicted of causing Seles grievous bodily harm. He was wielding a knife with a 9-inch (23cm) blade and attacked her, according to his story, because he wanted to put

Monica Seles's wound is tended to after she was stabbed by spectator Günter Parche during a 1993 tennis match. He was convicted of causing Seles grievous bodily harm.

the number one Seles out of action so his favorite female tennis player, Steffi Graf, could assume the top spot. Because of Parche's diminished responsibility (he was deemed mentally incompetent), he received a two-year suspended sentence. Reporter Bruce Lowitt describes the effect of the stabbing on Seles: "Although doctors said Seles could resume competition in about three months, the emotional trauma of the attack kept her off the tour for more than two years."[82] Seles never returned to the high level of performance that she had achieved prior to the attack.

CROWD MENTALITY DOES NOT LEAD TO VIOLENCE

"Gatherings or crowds do not drive people mad or make them lose control. People at gatherings have a wide variety of personal agendas and typically only a small minority of people are willing to engage in violent behavior."—The Center for Problem-Oriented Policing

"Responses to the Problem of Spectator Violence in Stadiums." Center for Problem-Oriented Policing. www.popcenter.org/problems/spectator_violence3.

Potential Causes of Spectator Violence

Fans that identify and cheer for their teams can easily lose their focus and behave in ways that they otherwise would not. There are many reasons why this happens. What an individual alone would not think of doing may become more likely when crowd mentality and crowd excitability enter the picture. The crowd moves itself along in what sociologists have labeled an "emotional contagion." Crowds often generate their own energy and take on a mind of their own. Psychiatrist Sigmund Freud once explained: "People who are in a crowd act differently . . . from those who are thinking individually. The minds of the group . . . merge to form a way of thinking. Each member's enthusiasm would be increased as a result, and one becomes less aware of the true nature of one's actions."[83] People thus get caught up in the emotions of the moment and often suspend their own sense of right and wrong. It only takes a few instigators to lead the crowd into violence.

One of the biggest factors that may contribute to spectator violence and the crowd mentality is alcohol. Statistics reveal that nearly 40 percent of all concession income comes from the sale of beer and alcohol. Many sports experts believe that alcohol increases any tendency toward aggressiveness that a person may harbor. A nonintoxicated fan may be able to dismiss poor play, an irritating fan, and other factors, but alcohol lessens an individual's inhibitions. Writers Gorman and Weeks explain: "Therefore, competitive situations in which, for example, one group of fans is taunting another could very well end in a fight if either or both have been drinking excessively."[84]

YOUNG ATHLETES SHOULD BE PROTECTED FROM ABUSIVE PRACTICES

"Our laws do not allow children to work, certainly not for excessive hours per day, but parents and coaches push child athletes to the extreme physical and emotional limits."—CAPPAA: Athlete Safety First

"Lessons Learned from the Max Gilpin Tragedy." CAPPAA: Athlete Safety First. October 4, 2010. www.cappaa.com/lessons-learned-in-the-max-gilpin-case.

Even the size of the stadium and the air temperature can impact the potential for spectator violence. The warmer the air, for example, the more chance there is of violence, as fans get hot and impatient with the playing on the field. The importance of the game is another component: The bigger the rivalry, the bigger the chance of spectator violence. In addition, according to Canadian researcher Michael Smith: "If spectators perceive players' actions on the field as violent, they are more likely to engage in violent acts during and after games."[85]

Finally, the increasing costs of tickets can also affect spectator violence. Fred Engh, president of the National Alliance for Youth Sports, elaborates: "Spectators today pay out large sums of money to watch games and see their heroes perform. Consequently, they believe it is their right to be loud, obnoxious, and degrading. Even worse, many exhibit violent behavior that impairs the safety of others."[86]

Parents Behaving Badly

Another significant source of sports violence involves parents of youth athletes. Many American parents today are deeply involved with their children's sporting activities. Many encourage their children to play a wide variety of sports and then support them and cheer for their success. These parents normally behave appropriately at sporting events and do not allow their feelings and emotions to get out of control.

Some parents, however, can lose control and behave in an inappropriate and violent manner. *Washington Post* reporter Heather A. Dinich explains: "From Little League to the big leagues and at all level of youth sports in between . . . more and more parents are crossing the line between being good-natured supporters and overbearing, greedy, and even violent participants in their children's athletic careers."[87]

Thomas Junta was convicted of voluntary manslaughter after he beat a man to death over a disagreement at a youth hockey practice session.

Experts offer many reasons for such behavior. In some cases the prospect of fame and fortune for their children makes parents lose all sense of perspective on the sidelines. Youth experts Dennis M. Docheff and James H. Conn explain another reason: "Youth sports generate a forum where parents struggle to balance their paternal [and maternal] instincts with their hunger for victory. . . . Many parents live vicariously through their children and view their child's youth sport performance as a direct reflection upon the standing of the entire family within the community."[88]

Perhaps the most extreme incident of parental violence occurred in 2000 in Massachusetts during a practice hockey session. Thomas Junta faced manslaughter charges for allegedly beating another parent to death in a dispute over rough play. Junta yelled at and berated his son for having failed to stick up for himself when another boy pushed him around. When another father suggested that the man ease up, he punched the man. Later, after the practice was over, Junta beat the man to death in the lobby of the rink in front of the children and other parents. This was believed to be the nation's first instance of a fatality involving parental violence. Junta was later convicted of voluntary manslaughter. Such incidents are now referred to as "Little League parent syndrome" or "parental rink rage." Such behavior may be on the rise and at times out of control at youth sporting events. In a survey done by *SportingKid* magazine in 2005, researchers questioned over three thousand parents, coaches, administrators, and players about parental violence. The survey showed that 84 percent of those questioned had witnessed parents acting in a violent manner at youth sporting events.

In another violent incident a parent poisoned eight players, aged twelve to fourteen, of a rival youth football team in Las Vegas in November 2000. All survived but were violently ill and hospitalized. In another instance a soccer father punched a fourteen-year-old boy in the face because he believed the player had pushed his son around. In California a parent was charged with misdemeanor child abuse after body slamming a thirteen-year-old football player who delivered a late hit on his son. One explanation for such behavior may be that when a parent believes their child has been harmed or harassed, they can find it very

Players Clash with Spectators

All too often, violent incidents occur between the players and the fans at sporting events. In December 1979, for example, a Boston Bruins hockey player was hit in the face by an object thrown from the stands. Several Boston players went into the stands to fight with the fans; one player removed a shoe from a fan and beat him with it. In 1995 Houston Rockets professional basketball player Vernon Maxwell entered the stands and punched a fan who had been heckling him.

One of the most well-known incidents, however, occurred in Detroit on November 19, 2004, during a National Basketball Association (NBA) game between the Indiana Pacers and the Detroit Pistons. A brawl on the court began when Ron Artest of the Pacers fouled Pistons player Ben Wallace. Wallace shoved Artest, leading to an altercation near the scorer's table. One Pistons fan threw a cup of beer at Artest, hitting him. Artest jumped into the front-row seats and confronted the wrong fan. This action eventually erupted into a brawl between Pistons fans and several of the Pacers. Artest then returned to the court, where he punched another Pistons fan who was taunting him. The fight caused a stoppage of the game with less than a minute to play. Pacers coach Rick Carlisle later said: "I felt like I was fighting for my life out there."[1] Pistons coach Larry Brown said it was the ugliest thing he had ever seen as both a coach and a player.

Artest was suspended for the rest of the season (seventy-three regular games and thirteen playoff games), and two of his teammates were suspended as well. Artest's suspension was the longest nondrug- or betting-related suspension in NBA history. Eight other players from both teams were also suspended. Several of the fans were charged with assault and banned for life from attending further events at the arena. Artest lost about $7 million in salary due to the suspension.

When asked about what may have caused this incident, sports psychologist Richard Ginsburg stated: "We're living in a fast-paced, impulse-driven culture, and I think fans, the players all want a quick fix. When you don't get that, you explode."[2]

1. Quoted in "Artest, Jackson Charge Palace Stands." ESPN.com. November 21, 2004. http://sports.espn.go.com/nba/news/story?id=1927380.
2. Quoted in Kevin Rothstein. "Violence in Sports Called Sign of Times." *Boston Herald*, November 23, 2004.

hard not to intervene. Chuck Nevius, a *San Francisco Chronicle* columnist, describes his own personal experience: "I've seen my kids knocked over. And it's very hard not to get that protective urge to kick in."[89]

Brawls also occur that involve parents, fans, and players. During a youth football game in California in the late 1990s, for example, the game erupted into a brawl that involved over one hundred players, coaches, parents, and spectators. Another brawl broke out in Florida during a youth basketball game. In this altercation involving parents, fans, and players, a pregnant woman was knocked to the floor, a referee suffered an ankle injury, and seven players had to be treated for a variety of cuts and bruises. Youth sports expert Engh elaborates: "The age-old ideal that children's sports should be fun and should contribute to physical development and social skills has been buried amid a plethora of police reports, emergency room visits, and arrest warrants."[90]

STRENUOUS PRACTICES ARE IMPORTANT IN TRAINING

"If a man is a quitter, I'd rather find out in practice than in a game. I ask for all a player has so I'll know later what I can expect."—Paul "Bear" Bryant, former University of Alabama football coach

Quoted in Brad Winters. "Leadership Quotes by Coach Bear Bryant." Coach Like a Pro. www.coachlikeapro.com/coach-paul-bear-bryant.html.

Many of these violent acts perpetrated by parents are being directed at the referees and umpires who officiate at their children's sporting events. The National Association of Sports Officials reported in 2004 that the organization receives over one hundred reports each year about violent incidents directed at referees and umpires. The organization admitted that this was probably only a fraction of the offenses committed against officials; the majority of incidents are not reported. Jim Ferguson, the state president of the Virginia Soccer Association, agrees. He reported that the Virginia Youth Soccer Association handled between fifteen and twenty cases of assault and abuse directed at referees during the years 1997 to 2000. Another example comes from a 1994 survey taken in Ohio of baseball and softball umpires that revealed that 84 out of 782 respondents had suffered physical assaults at least once in their career. Most were minor assaults, but a few involved hitting umpires with baseball bats. Twenty-one states have passed legislation that protects officials from violence by prosecuting offenders. Many referees have become so concerned over parental violence that they have started buying assault insurance.

Coaches: Not Always Good Role Models

In addition to parents and spectators, coaches at all levels of sports can also be guilty of violent acts. This can have tragic consequences, since coaches often set the stage for how their players, and even fans, behave. Bob Marshaus of Clinton, Maryland, is a veteran basketball referee and in 2000 was commissioner of the Maryland Basketball Officials Association. He stated: "I'm a firm believer that everything stems from the coach. If the coach yells at an official, he's like a cheerleader. Fans see that, and they start screaming at officials."[91]

An example of a coach or manager inciting the fans occurred in Cincinnati in 1988. The Cincinnati Reds baseball team was playing the New York Mets when the umpire made a disputed call. Reds manager Pete Rose stormed from the dugout and engaged in a shouting and shoving match with the umpire; he was ejected from the game. Fans responded by turning ugly; for fifteen minutes they threw objects on the field, aiming at the umpires. Beer and soda bottles were the main weapons; the violence was severe enough to cause the umpires to flee the field. Rose was later suspended for thirty days for instigating the violence.

In many cases the coach is expected, and occasionally encouraged, by athletic directors to be hot tempered and violent. The name of Bobby Knight, a former college basketball coach, immediately comes to the mind of most sports fans when someone mentions such coaches. Considered a brilliant coach who led his teams to an amazing 902 victories and three NCAA basketball championships, Knight was, sadly, better known for his antics on and off the court. ESPN writers elaborate: "He was a brilliant coach, but he was also a raging, foul-mouthed bully who'd made headlines for punching a player, fighting a cop, throwing a fan into a trash can, tossing a chair onto the court in the middle of a game."[92]

The name of Woody Hayes, longtime coach of the Ohio State Buckeyes, also comes to mind when thinking of violent coaches. Hayes, according to most sports analysts, was an excellent coach who led his team to five national championships. But Hayes also had a hot temper that often got out of control. ESPN writers explain: "Over the years, he punched players, a cameraman, an assistant coach, a goal post. Then in the Gator Bowl in 1978, he punched a Clemson player named Charlie Bauman who had the audacity to intercept a Buckeye pass in the final minutes of a close game."[93] Despite his winning record, Ohio State athletic officials asked Hayes to resign; when he refused, the coach was fired. However, not long after his firing, Hayes was given an award for sportsmanship and character building by the College Football Hall of Fame.

Ohio State coach Woody Hayes was known for his volatile temper. He punched players, coaches, cameramen, and goal posts. Finally, after being televised punching a Clemson player as well as one of his own at the 1978 Gator Bowl, the university fired him.

Some coaches are also guilty of abusing their own players. One of the more recent noteworthy incidents involved football coach Mike Leach of Texas Tech. In a highly publicized case, Leach was accused of confining player Adam Jones to an equipment room after Jones received a concussion during a game. Already being watched by the university for refusing to sign new guidelines on coaching behavior, Leach was fired by the college president and athletic director. Among the guidelines that the university cited in his dismissal were: "Decisions regarding whether an injury warrants suspension for practice or play will be determined by a physician. . . . There will be no retaliation against any student who has suffered an injury."[94]

Football coaches have also been involved in an increasing number of players' deaths. These deaths have occurred during practice sessions and are generally a result of heat exhaustion. In a recent incident involving a high school athlete, the coach was brought to court on charges. *Sports Illustrated* reporter Thomas Lake explains: "Three days after he collapsed from heatstroke at practice in 2008, fifteen-year-old Max Gilpin became one of at least 665 boys since 1931 to die as a result of high school football. Here is what made his case different: The Commonwealth of Kentucky tried to prove Max's coach, Jason Stimson, had a hand in killing him."[95] While the coach was eventually exonerated, the prosecutor of the Stimson case hoped the trial would encourage other coaches to rethink how their practices were run. Louisville, Kentucky, high school coach Ty Scroggins took the message to heart. "I used to be one of the crazy coaches, running around, slapping the guys in the head and getting them motivated. I've pretty much stopping doing some of this stuff."[96]

This trial also brought to light the number of tragic deaths that all too often occur because of demanding training sessions. Some football coaches at all levels of play require lengthy and arduous training sessions in all kinds of weather. Paul "Bear" Bryant, longtime winning coach at the University of Alabama, was well known for his aggressive practices. Bryant's goal was to produce tough football players who could endure the worst physical strain. He showed no mercy on the practice field, as Lake describes: "Players who collapsed from heat exhaustion

Texas Tech University's head football coach Mike Leach was fired for confining a player to an equipment room after the player said he could not practice because he had received a concussion.

had to crawl to the sideline or be dragged off by student assistants. When a boy fell face-first to the ground from heatstroke, Bryant kicked his fallen body."[97]

Some coaches maintain that strenuous practices produce stronger athletes who do not tire or underperform during important games. In addition, some players are so committed to being part of a football team that they push themselves to the extreme to show their commitment to the sport. Some sports experts agree that hard practices are acceptable as long as the players are monitored for problems throughout the experience. Other sociologists and sports experts contend, however, that such coaching behavior is not only negligent but violent and abusive, as well as being extremely dangerous for players of all ages.

Sports have become associated with many kinds of violence: sanctioned and unsanctioned violence between players, off-the-field violence, and violent acts committed by spectators, parents, and coaches. As some observers warn that violence is on the rise throughout the sports world, a number of sociologists, psychologists, and other sports experts are determinedly trying to find ways to prevent and end such acts.

REDUCTION AND PREVENTION OF VIOLENCE IN SPORTS

Numerous problems involving violence have been identified in athletics. Sports experts, sociologists, and psychologists continue to evaluate and examine these problems, searching for ways to reduce, control, and/or prevent violence in sports. Areas that are being examined include violence on the playing field at all levels of sports, spectator violence, and off-the-field violence, along with the question whether the legal system should become involved in incidents involving sports violence.

Programs Aimed at Stopping Violence at Youth Sporting Events

There have been some steps taken in youth sports to reduce and ultimately prevent violence. In Jupiter, Florida, for instance, Jeff Leslie, president of the Jupiter Tequesta Athletic Association, took action to force parents to curb their acts of violence. The Jupiter Association, in fact, became the first youth sports organization to require parents to attend classes in sportsmanship. While in class, parents were asked to sign a code of ethics, promising to promote fair play and control any violent tendencies. If the parents refused to attend the class or sign the code, their children were not allowed to participate in any sporting activities. Fred Engh, parent and president of the nonprofit National Alliance for Youth Sports in West Palm Beach, Florida, advocates that all youth sports groups follow the example of the Jupiter Association. He states: "No organization that runs sports for children should allow parents to

Fred Engh, president and CEO of the National Alliance for Youth Sports, believes that no sports organization should allow a child to register until the child's parents attend a training program on ethics and sportsmanship.

register their child without the parent going through an orientation and training program on ethics and sportsmanship."[98] These organizations believe that any significant change must begin with the parents. By offering sportsmanship classes, the organizations hope to persuade parents to provide a positive role model for their young athlete offspring.

In addition to offering sportsmanship classes, some sociologists and psychologists contend that athletic leagues should also have "zero tolerance" policies. According to these policies, if parents misbehave, their child would be suspended from play; for second or third incidents, their child would be removed from the team. In addition, some leagues are beginning to enact fines for abusive or violent parents. If parents fail to pay the fine, their children are not allowed to play.

Not all youth organizations or parents believe that such steps are necessary. In some cases the leagues rely on the referees and other officials to pinpoint problematic parents and deal with them in an appropriate manner. Parents who habitually cause problems can also be reported to the youth organization. It is then up to the organization to take steps with these individuals to curb violent behavior.

It is also absolutely essential, some sociologists say, that players should be educated from the earliest possible age about what is and is not acceptable in athletics. Richard Lapchick, founder of Northeastern University's Center for the Study of Sport in Society, elaborates: "The sooner you get to them, the better off they'll be, either to stop themselves or to intervene in a case where violence is happening."[99] Educating players at the youth level about the differences between sanctioned and unsanctioned violence could help mitigate the use of excessive violence in collegiate and professional sports.

BEANBALLS SHOULD BE SEVERELY PENALIZED

"Pitchers need the inside of the plate and they should get it. But if they throw at a batter's head, they should be tossed, fined, suspended, and made to do service in a brain-trauma unit."—Rick Telander, *Chicago Sun Times* journalist

Rick Telander. "Was Frank Robinson's Ruling Too Harsh?" *Chicago Sun Times*, April 28, 2000.

Another program dedicated to ending youth sports violence by reintroducing sportsmanship to athletics is the Positive Coaching Alliance, an organization that conducts live and online workshops for coaches, parents, and youth sports groups. Jim Thompson, the founder and executive director, explains that one of the methods the alliance uses is initiating conversation about controversial issues in sports and violent incidents viewed on television. Thompson explains that such incidents are "teachable moments, talkable moments. If you're watching a football game with your kids, and a player steps on the head of another player, that's an opportunity to express your values."[100]

In addition to requiring parents to attend sportsmanship programs, many youth leagues are also instituting a code of ethics that coaches must sign. These codes, according to the National Alliance for Youth Sports, emphasize that coaches should place the emotional and physical well-being of their players ahead of any personal desire to win. Some sports psychologists

Fair Play Code

In an effort to decrease violence among young athletes, many youth leagues today are requiring parents to attend sportsmanship classes and sign a code of ethics. One such code, written for hockey, appears on the Canadian Centres for Teaching Peace website:

For Parents:

I will not force my child to participate in hockey.

I will remember that my child plays hockey for his or her enjoyment; not mine.

I will encourage my child to play by the rules and to resolve conflict without resorting to hostility or violence.

I will teach my child that doing one's best is as important as winning so that my child will never feel defeated by the outcome of a game.

I will make my child feel like a winner every time by offering praise.

I will never ridicule or yell at my child for making a mistake or losing a game.

I will remember that children learn best by example. I will applaud good plays and performances by both my child's team and their opponents.

I will never question the official's judgment or honesty in public.

I will support all efforts to remove verbal and physical abuse from children's hockey games.

I will respect and show appreciation for the volunteer coaches who give their time to coach hockey for my child.

"Sports: When Winning Is the Only Thing, Can Violence Be Far Away?" Canadian Centres for Teaching Peace. www.peace.ca/sports/htm.

also suggest that any attempt by the coach to encourage young athletes to perform violent acts should be penalized and, if necessary, such a coach should be removed. Child experts also believe that coaches should be strictly scrutinized about their practice sessions; coaches who run aggressive and abusive practices, they feel, should be closely watched and reprimanded or fired as needed. Many experts believe that coaches should treat each player as an individual, lead by example, display fair play and sportsmanship at all times, and provide a safe playing situation for their players.

Some experts, however, contend that in many instances, especially at the high school and collegiate levels, coaches are merely trying to deliver what they have been paid to create—winning teams. At the college level, in particular, each year sees a number of coaches being fired for having a losing record. School administrators also know that a winning coach will bring in scholarship money and more financing for their athletic programs. Thus, many administrators are willing to look the other way when complaints are made about an abusive or aggressive coach. Collegiate athletes also tend to tolerate such abuse if they are part of a winning team. It has, for instance, been well documented by sports experts that Bobby Knight bullied his players and sometimes treated them in an abusive way. Yet most of his former players admire and respect the coach and claim that he taught them well. Isiah Thomas played for Knight at Indiana University in the 1980s and went on to become an all-star National Basketball Association (NBA) player and coach; he elaborates: "You know there were times, when if I had had a gun, I think I would have shot him. And there were other times when I wanted to put my arms around him, hug him, and tell him that I loved him."[101]

Are Fines and Suspensions Enough?

On the professional and collegiate level, the majority of sports experts contend that too many of the players who commit acts of violence on the field are not facing the consequences of their actions. These experts maintain that the traditional punishment for violent acts, such as small fines and short suspensions, has not been sufficient to stop future acts. Sports stars who make millions of dollars a year are not intimidated by fines that rarely exceed a few thousand dollars.

These sports experts instead believe that players who commit acts of unsanctioned violence on the field must be held more responsible and accountable for their actions. The National Football League (NFL) is one sports organization that has seen a dramatic change in player violence in the last twenty years. *Sports*

Illustrated reporter Terry McDonell elaborates: "Football is experiencing a tougher scrutiny, and it started with the recognition among players and league officials that the violent hits and resultant injuries had gone way over the top."[102]

RETALIATION IS A NECESSARY PART OF SPORTS

"Violent retaliation serves ethical purposes. . . . Moral values instilled by violent retaliation [include] honor, deterrence of future violence, and team unity. . . . Violent retaliation preserves the honor of the sport and the team. By fighting back against an inappropriate violent act, the retribution tells the opposing athlete or team that games are about fairness." —Sean McAleer

Quoted in James C. Greening. "Ethical Implications of Violent Retaliation in Sports." Big Games, November 9, 2010. http://biggames.ning.com/profiles/blogs/ethical-implications-of-violent-retaliation-in-sport

When new NFL commissioner Roger Goodell took over for former commissioner Paul Tagliabue in late 2006, the punishment for violent hits began to change. In April 2007 Goodell announced a new and toughened policy. He stated: "Football is a tough game and we need to do everything possible to protect all players . . . from unnecessary injury caused by illegal and dangerous hits. . . . Any conduct that unnecessarily risks the safety of other players has no role in the game of football and will be disciplined at increased levels on a first offense."[103]

Goodell began to punish players by suspending them for much longer periods of time than had been used in the past. During these suspensions, professional football players are not paid; thus, they stand to lose a lot more money than in the past. This impacts them where it hurts the most—in the wallet. A number of professional football players did not agree with the new rules mandating longer suspensions. Longtime Baltimore Ravens defensive star Ray Lewis, for instance, is one player who believes there are now too many rules. He states: "My goodness. You can't do anything anymore. It's a tragedy. . . . There are just too many rules, man."[104]

In October 2010 Goodell's determination to protect the players was tested. Goodell and the NFL, alarmed by the number of concussions that were occurring in football, outlawed helmet-to-helmet hits. The NFL had seen an alarming number of concussions in 2010; 154 through the eighth week of the season, a 20 percent increase from 2009. Most of these injuries occurred because of helmet-to-helmet hits. The decision was made to ban these hits after a particularly violent weekend when a number of players left their games with concussions. The Pittsburgh Steelers' James Harrison hit two different Cleveland Browns players, causing head injuries to both. And the Philadelphia Eagles' DeSean Jackson and the Atlanta Falcons' Dunta Robinson were both knocked unconscious after a collision in which Robinson led with his head to make the tackle. These three players were fined a total of $175,000. Many critics, however, believe that even these fines were not sufficient. They contend that even the more expensive fines were no more than 1 or 2 percent of a player's annual salary.

For NFL commissioner Roger Goodell, addressing conduct that unnecessarily risks the safety of other players is a top priority. He has handed out large fines to players for violent hits.

Some professional football players disagree with these fines, stating that helmet-to-helmet hits are usually unintentional and should not be punished. Andre Johnson, a wide receiver for the Houston Texans, elaborates: "A lot of times, guys are just out there playing. . . . I don't really think they're thinking about the helmet-to-helmet contact."[105]

Another sport that has come under recent scrutiny for its violence is professional hockey. Since the beginning of the twenty-first century, however, the National Hockey League (NHL) has tried to curb some of the more vicious forms of unsanctioned violence seen on the ice, particularly hits to the head. The issue increased in importance following several blind-side hits, hits coming from an unseen attacker, on star players. On March 7, 2010, for instance, Boston Bruins center Marc Savard was hit in the head by Pittsburgh Penguins player Matt Cooke. Cooke came in from behind, raised his shoulder, and hit Savard in the head. No pen-

Eagles' DeSean Jackson, left, and Falcons' Dunta Robinson, center, reel backward after an especially violent collision that left both players injured. Because Robinson led with his helmet he received a heavy fine.

Marc Savard of the Boston Bruins lies incapacitated on the ice after being blindsided by Pittsburgh Penguins' Matt Cooke. Although Savard had a concussion and was out of the game for two months, Cooke received no penalty or fine.

alty was called; nor was Cooke suspended. Savard ended up with a concussion that kept him out of the game for two months.

That hit and others led in March 2010 to a meeting of hockey general managers; the topic on the agenda was concussions, head hits, and blind shots. After deliberation, the managers voted to ban blind-side hits to the head, defining such hits as any play where a player's head is targeted by another player coming from the first player's blind side. NHL commissioner Gary Bettman stated: "We believe this is the right thing to do for the game and for the safety of our players. The elimination of these types of hits should significantly reduce the number of injuries, including concussions, without adversely affecting the level of physicality in the game."[106] The NHL Players' Association also voted to approve the changes, admitting that such hits had become a concern for players as well. St. Louis Blues' player Jay McClement spoke for many hockey players when he stated: "Nobody wants to have the serious injuries in the game, and nobody wants those long-term or career-ending injuries. I think more than anything it's going to make guys think twice about how they finish their plays."[107]

Some sportswriters believe that, even with the new rules in football and hockey, unsanctioned violence will be difficult to eliminate. Writer Coakley agrees: "Once violence is built into the culture, structures, and strategies of a sport, controlling or eliminating it is difficult."[108] Coakley also recommends that not just players should be punished for on-the-field violence. He contends, as do a number of other sports experts, that coaches and team owners should also be fined for player misconduct.

Stopping Spectator Violence

In addition to punishing acts of violence among players, in recent years many efforts have also been made to reduce spectator violence. One of the steps taken has been to control alcohol sales at sporting venues. Many stadiums have instituted alcohol-free zones, while others have prohibited beer sales during the late innings or late stages of games in the hopes that fans will have more time to sober up before leaving a sporting event. Most stadiums and arenas have also outlawed glass containers to prevent their use as projectiles thrown onto the field or floor.

EACH SPORT SHOULD POLICE THEIR OWN ATHLETES

"I say that [sports should police their own athletes] because I believe the leagues are doing a very good job at meting out appropriate penalties."—Mel Narol, sports lawyer for the National Association of Sports Officials

Quoted in *Christian Science Monitor.* "When Sports Violence Is a Criminal Act." February 28, 2000.

Fistfights in the stands between strangers and even between friends are almost an everyday occurrence in sports. In fact, nearly one-third of fans suffer some type of unpleasant experience when they attend sporting events. These experiences range from someone pouring a drink on them to indecent exposure, being insulted, or being spit upon. Today many athletic arenas have encouraged fans to call posted phone numbers to report disruptive individuals in the stands. In Milwaukee, at the Brewers' stadium, for instance, fans know that if they become disorderly they will be immediately ejected.

In addition, more and more stadiums are hiring extra security personnel. Some security people even work undercover in an effort to pinpoint problem drinkers and disruptive fans. Heightened police presence at the end of games is also more common. The presence of police and security guards prohibit fans from streaming onto the field or court after a game as they

The Call for Closer Officiating

Many sports experts suggest that closer officiating during athletic events could help reduce violence. In baseball, for instance, when a pitcher intentionally hits a batter, umpires are now acting to punish such incidents. If an umpire believes the pitcher is throwing deliberately at another player, the pitcher is first given a warning. If he continues to throw such pitches, he is ejected from the game and fined. So are opposing pitchers who try to retaliate. While this has not completely eliminated such tactics, many experts feel such ejections and fines are a big step in the right direction.

Dean Smith, former basketball coach of the University of North Carolina Tar Heels, believes that both college and professional basketball could benefit from closer officiating. Smith writes:

> Most veteran coaches I know are alarmed with the roughness of the game today. Two of the greatest names in basketball history—John Wooden [legendary college coach] and Bill Bradley [NBA player]—not long ago were asked what they see as current trends in basketball, and what worries them most about the game's future. They each

said they are alarmed by how much the officials let go in today's game.[1]

Smith believes that officials should be instructed by their supervisors to call all fouls to keep games from getting too rough or out of control. In fact, he suggests that the National Collegiate Athletic Association (NCAA) hire full-time officials for college basketball games. Smith explains: "Such a system would give supervisors control over their officials. If officials didn't call the game the way it was meant to be called, the supervisors could dismiss them."[2] Instead, most of the men and women who work as officials in college basketball have full-time jobs outside the sport. This is true in football as well, where officials are often inconsistent in calling penalties for violent acts. While it is often difficult to separate a sanctioned hit from a cheap shot, referees have come under criticism for not calling enough penalties. The National Football League does sanction officials from time to time for errors made during a game.

1. Dean Smith with John Kilgo and Sally Jenkins. *A Coach's Life.* New York: Random House, 1999, p. 276.
2. Smith. *A Coach's Life,* p. 278.

once did, at least in professional sports. In addition, high-tech surveillance systems are being utilized at many large sports complexes, while protective tunnels, walls, and other barriers are being used to shield players from fan access. In addition, most stadiums and other sports arenas now utilize metal detectors; fans are also searched prior to entering stadiums. Officials have been amazed at some of the weapons that have been confiscated. Hammers, chains, darts, guns, smoke bombs, grenades, black-jacks (a short, leather-covered club), and knives have all been found on fans entering the stadium.

In addition, in international soccer—known to the rest of the world as football—the Football Spectators Act of 1989 allows courts to impose permanent expulsion for those fans who have been found guilty of hooliganism. This means those particular spectators are not allowed to attend sporting events at particular stadiums and venues. Many American professional teams are also taking similar stances against troublemakers. Despite these attempts, incidents still occur.

Some critics of spectator behavior also assert that the police must become more involved in instances where spectators act in a violent manner. Said a Queens, New York, district attorney: "We seek jail against them [unruly fans] . . . they just spoil the game for the rest of us. They deserve incarceration as well as ejection."[109] These comments followed the sentencing of a New York Mets fan in 1986 to fifteen days in jail for fighting with security guards.

A number of sports experts also agree that urban athletic administrators at the high school and college level need to improve their relationship with local police, school police, and security forces. Journalist Donald Collins elaborates:

> Administrators can usually predict problems they'll confront in their gyms in advance. They know or should know which spectators have a history of violence or have scores to settle, and which neighborhoods have rivalries. Armed with that knowledge, they can take steps to minimize the risk of violence as much as possible, such as using a metal detector . . . and by having enough security personnel on site for crowd control.[110]

Despite the increased violence from spectators, some owners are still reluctant to deal with fans who get out of hand. They are fearful that such fans will stop coming to the ballpark or arena.

Low attendance would mean less revenue and profit, something that owners and sports management groups take into consideration when making decisions about punishing fans.

Should Unsanctioned Violence Be the Province of the Police?

With the police often helping to reduce spectator violence, some sports experts are questioning whether the police need to be involved in acts of violence committed by the athletes themselves. The police and court system, for the most part, have been very reluctant to get involved in incidents of violence on the playing field. The belief was that what happened on the field should be dealt with on the field. Even in cases where players were severely injured by unsanctioned violence, those players were reluctant to testify or press charges against an aggressor. Part of the difficulty in prosecuting players is that it is often difficult for law enforcement actually to prove that an act of violence was an intentional act with the purpose of causing injury.

After being charged with assault for his attack on Donald Brashear, NHL player Marty McSorely, right, was given a record fine and a suspension in addition to eighteen months of probation.

Law enforcement is beginning to emerge as a solution to unsanctioned violence, however. Richard Lapchick, director of the Center for the Study of Sport in Society at Northeastern University, elaborates: "For whatever reason, sport has had a kind of sanctuary atmosphere to it in terms of the legal system and police have kept a distance . . . [but] the public has gotten fed up with athletes crossing violent lines, both on and off the court, and that may contribute to police entering the sanctuary."[111]

Canada has often been more willing to bring charges against athletes for violence during sporting events than the United States. The first criminal case in Canada, in fact, occurred in 1969 and involved a fight between two hockey players. Both faced assault charges but were ultimately acquitted. Few of the initial cases brought guilty verdicts.

THE LEAGUES CANNOT POLICE VIOLENCE

"If the leagues are doing such a good job policing themselves, why does the violence persist?" —*Christian Science Monitor* editors

Christian Science Monitor. "When Sports Violence Is a Criminal Act." February 28, 2000.

Guilty verdicts became more common in the early twenty-first century. Boston Bruins defenseman Marty McSorley was charged with assault with a deadly weapon after an on-ice incident on February 21, 2000. McSorley attacked Vancouver Canucks player Donald Brashear with his stick; Brashear was struck in the head and immediately dropped unconscious to the ice, suffering a severe concussion. McSorley was suspended by the NHL for the remainder of the season (twenty-three games) and the playoffs. It was the harshest penalty ever imposed by the league up to that time. He was also charged with assault by the Vancouver police and faced up to eighteen months in jail. McSorley was found guilty of the charges and placed on eighteen months of probation. Following the conviction, the NHL suspended McSorley for an additional year; McSorley never played another game.

In another hockey incident, Minnesota North Stars' Dino Ciccarelli was sentenced to one day in jail and fined one thousand dollars for striking Toronto defenseman Luke Richardson several times in the head with his stick. And in the most recent incident, Vancouver Canuck Todd Bertuzzi was charged with assault after punching another player in the head with his fist, causing a concussion and other injuries. He pleaded guilty and was placed on twelve months of probation and eighty hours of community service by a Vancouver court.

The United States has been more efficient in bringing charges against nonprofessional athletes. Tony Limon, for instance, was a star on his San Antonio high school basketball team. After elbowing and breaking an opponent's nose during a game in his senior season, he was sentenced to five years in prison for assault.

Journalists for the *Christian Science Monitor* conclude: "Now, as violence in many sports is becoming more prevalent and public patience with it less so, police and prosecutors are edging toward taking action on the ice, gridiron, and . . . courts."[112]

Curbing Off-the-Field Violence

In addition to questioning whether law enforcement needs to be involved in sports violence, experts also question the efforts being made to curb off-the-field violence perpetrated by athletes. Many sports leagues, for example, are increasingly using counseling, fines, and the threat of suspension to deter players from violent crime. Addressing the problem among professional football players, former NFL commissioner Paul Tagliabue stated: "New programs were begun in 1997. . . . New penalties for alcohol abuse, as well as league-wide counseling, anger-prevention programs, and treatment have helped lower crime statistics among players."[113] Many critics contended, however, that the NFL still was not doing enough.

When Roger Goodell took over from Tagliabue, the situation began to change. Prior to his being named commissioner, and despite the new player conduct codes, no player had ever been suspended for more than four games. One of Goodell's first acts was to suspend Atlanta Falcons quarterback Michael Vick indefinitely for his role in dogfighting and dog abuse charges. Since that time, Goodell has continued his aggressive suspensions; he suspended Adam "Pacman" Jones for the entire 2007 season, Chris Henry for the first half of a season, and Tank Johnson for half a season; all for a variety of run-ins with the law. Henry, who was turning his life around, was tragically killed in an automobile accident in December 2009. Other professional sports leagues are also using larger fines and longer suspensions to deal with similar problems in their sports.

Many colleges and universities are also beginning to take small steps to reduce violence committed by athletes on campus, particularly sexual violence. When a collegiate athlete or other student is charged with sexual assault or rape, a few universities are

NFL commissioner Roger Goodell suspended Adam "Pacman" Jones of the Tennessee Titans for an entire season because of his numerous run-ins with the law.

now beginning to apply academic punishments, with penalties including suspension from school for a period of time or outright expulsion.

Only a minority of colleges, however, actually impose any sanctions on the athletic team, the coach, or the athletic director. Many female advocates hope this will eventually change. The National Coalition Against Violent Athletes is one organization working to further address the issue of sexual assault on campus by making efforts to ensure that offending athletes are held accountable for their actions. Some sociologists and psychologists believe that universities need to do more to prevent the crimes and violence in the first place. According to these experts, the first step should be creating an awareness of the issue of sexual assault itself. Secondly, universities need to improve communication so that the issue can be discussed openly on campus. Thirdly, efforts should be made to educate all student-athletes, coaches, and administrators about the frequency of sexual assault. Finally, coaches and athletic administrators must model the proper respect for women through their own behavior.

One program to curb violence and sexual abuse is the Mentors in Violence Prevention (MVP) program. Jackson Katz, one of the cofounders of the program, describes how MVP helps: "The MVP program was designed to train male college and high school student-athletes and other student leaders to use their status to speak out against rape, battering, sexual harassment, gay bashing, and all other forms of sexist abuse and violence."[114]

Some sports experts are now suggesting that in order to curb collegiate sports violence, universities investigate a high school athlete's criminal past prior to the school offering scholarships. In 2010 *Sports Illustrated* and CBS Sports did a study of high school football recruits to the top twenty-five college football preseason teams. The survey, published in March 2011, showed that 7 percent of the high school athletes had criminal records; 40 percent of those for serious offenses such as assault and battery, burglary, and sexual assault. NCAA president Mark Emmert addressed the seriousness of these statistics: "It is a set of facts that obviously should concern all of us . . . 7%, that's way too high. I think 2% is too high. . . . You certainly don't want a large number of people with criminal backgrounds involved in activities that represent the NCAA."[115]

While some college administrators believe that scholarships should never be given to athletes with criminal records, a number of coaches disagree. Writers George Dohrmann and Jeff Benedict explain: "They [the coaches] know that not every kid—or every crime—is the same. . . . It would lessen the sport's power to change lives."[116] These coaches believe that college sports and the university atmosphere can help athletes find meaning and purpose in life and lead them away from lives of crime.

The use of unsanctioned violence in sports may remain a contentious issue for years to come. More research is needed in many areas: the long-term physical effects of on-the-field violence; the possible relationship between on-field violence and off-field violence; the impact of a winning-at-all costs attitude; the incidence of sports rage and retaliation; and the reasons for violence by spectators, coaches, and parents. Further measures in these areas may one day be used to dramatically reduce, control, or prevent sports violence.

Introduction: A Worldwide Phenomenon

1. Quoted in Robert M. Gorman and David Weeks. *Death at the Ballpark: A Comprehensive Study of Game-Related Fatalities of Players, Other Personnel and Spectators in Amateur and Professional Baseball: 1862–2007.* Jefferson, NC: McFarland, 2009, p. 81.
2. Dawn Comstock. "Prevalence of Sports-Related Violence Increasing." Nationwide Children's Hospital, January 13, 2006. www.newswise.com/articles/view/517287.
3. Lynn M. Jamieson and Thomas J. Orr. *Sport and Violence: A Critical Examination of Sport.* Burlington, MA: Butterworth-Heinemann, 2009, p. 4.
4. Jay Coakley. *Sports in Society: Issues and Controversies.* Boston: McGraw-Hill, 2007, p. 153.
5. John H. Kerr. *Rethinking Aggression and Violence in Sport.* London: Routledge, 2005, p. 7.
6. Quoted in Viv Saunders. "Sport and 20th Century American Society." *History Review*, March, 2010.
7. Saunders. "Sport and 20th Century American Society."
8. Jamieson and Orr. *Sport and Violence*, p. 1.
9. Jamieson and Orr. *Sport and Violence*, p. 1.

Chapter 1: Violence in Sports— Sanctioned and Unsanctioned

10. Quoted in Jabari Ritchie. "The Fun and the Fury: An Increase in Violence Surrounding Youth Sports Sends Parents and Officials Looking for Answers to Stem Disturbing Tide." *Minneapolis Star-Tribune*, August 22, 2001.
11. Jonathan Hardcastle. "Sports Violence." Ezine Articles. http://ezinearticles.com/?Sports-Violence&id=290850.

12. Rit Nosotro. "Violence in Sports: Today's Gladiator Attitude." HyperHistory.net. www.hyperhistory.net/apwh/essays/comp/cw32violentsports.htm.

13. Quoted in Jamieson and Orr. *Sport and Violence*, p. 32.

14. Quoted in Kerr. *Rethinking Aggression and Violence in Sport*, p. 67.

15. Josephson Institute. "Frequently Asked Questions." http://josephsoninstitute.org/sports/overview/faq.html.

16. Quoted in Thomas Tutko. *Winning Is Everything and Other American Myths*. New York: MacMillian, 1976, p. 18.

17. Sean McClelland. "At Least She Didn't Hit Her with a Foreign Object." *Dayton (OH) Daily News*, March 6, 2010, p. B2.

18. McClelland. "At Least She Didn't Hit Her with a Foreign Object," p. B2.

19. Gorman and Weeks. *Death at the Ballpark*, p. 1.

20. Fred Engh. *Why Johnny Hates Sports*. New York: Avery, 1999, p. 16.

21. Engh. *Why Johnny Hates Sports*, p. 16.

22. Kerr. *Rethinking Aggression and Violence in Sport*, p. xii.

23. Quoted in "Research on the Effects of Media Violence." Media Awareness Network. www.media-awareness.ca/english/issues/violence/effects_media_violence.cfm.

24. Quoted in "Research on the Effects of Media Violence."

25. Michael S. James and Tracy Ziemer. "Are Youth Athletes Becoming Bad Sports?" ABC News, August 8, 2000. http://abcnews.go.com/Sports/story?id=99665.

26. Jamieson and Orr. *Sport and Violence*, p. 97.

Chapter 2: Fostering Violence Through Competition and Aggression

27. Jamieson and Orr. *Sport and Violence*, p. 164.

28. Kerr. *Rethinking Aggression and Violence in Sport*, p. 61.

29. Kerr. *Rethinking Aggression and Violence in Sport*, p. 52.

30. Canadian Centres for Teaching Peace. "Sports: When Winning Is the Only Thing, Can Violence Be Far Away?" December 8, 2004. www.peace.ca/sports.htm.

31. Quoted in Tutko. *Winning Is Everything and Other American Myths*, p. 4.

32. Quoted in Engh. *Why Johnny Hates Sports*, p. 27.

33. Engh. *Why Johnny Hates Sports*, p. 27.

34. Canadian Centres for Teaching Peace. "Sports."

35. Carlton Kendrick. "Teaching Good Sportsmanship." Family Education. http://life.familyeducation.com/sports/parenting/36484.html.

36. Larry M. Lance and Charlynn E. Ross. "Views of Violence in American Sports: A Study of College Students." *College Student Journal*, June 2000. http://findarticles.com/p/articles/mi_mOFCR/is_2_34/ai_63365174.

37. Jamieson and Orr. *Sport and Violence*, p. 72.

38. Coakley. *Sports in Society*, p. 203.

39. Coakley. *Sports in Society*, p. 202.

40. Quoted in Kerr. *Rethinking Aggression and Violence in Sport*, p. ii.

41. Coakley. *Sports in Society*, p. 202.

42. Quoted in Lars Anderson. "Motor Mouth." *Sports Illustrated*, July 5, 2010, p. 60.

43. Quoted in Kevin Quinn. "Violence Has Become a Part of the American Sports Culture." *Marist News Watch*, Spring 2003. www.academic.marist.edu/mwwatch/spring03/articles/Sports/sportsfinal.html.

44. Sergio Bonilla. "Pitchers Hitting Batters as Retaliation: An Old Time Tradition." Suite101. www.suite101.com/content/pitchers-hitting-batters-as-retaliation-an-old-time-tradition-a264692.

45. Quoted in Coakley. *Sports in Society*, p. 207.

46. Quoted in Mike Bresnahan. "Moore Not Ready to Forgive Bertuzzi." *Cincinnati Post*, March 20, 2004.

47. Quoted Kerr. *Rethinking Aggression and Violence in Sport*, p. 72.

48. Christine Nucci and Young-Shim Kim. "Improving Socialization Through Sport: An Analytical Review of Literature on Aggression and Sportsmanship." *Physical Educator*, September 22, 2005.

49. Engh. *Why Johnny Hates Sports*, p. 5.

50. Kerr. *Rethinking Aggression and Violence in Sport*, p. 85.

Chapter 3: The Spillover of Sports Violence: Off-the-Field Violence

51. Mike Imrem. "Does Violence in Sports Transfer to Homestead?" *Arlington Heights (IL) Daily Herald*, July 26, 2002.

52. Quoted in Coakley. *Sports in Society*, p. 211.

53. Quoted in Coakley. *Sports in Society*, p. 211.

54. Quoted in Ciro Scotti. "Who Says Pro Athletes Have to Be Role Models?" *BusinessWeek*, November 24, 1998. www .businessweek.com/bwdaily/dnflash/nov1998/nf81124c.htm.

55. Quoted in *Morning Edition*. "Violence in the Personal Lives of Amateur Athletes." NPR, September 18, 1995.

56. Greg Couch. "No Denying Link Between Athletes and Guns." *Chicago Sun Times*, November 18, 2007.

57. Quoted in Couch. "No Denying Link Between Athletes and Guns."

58. Couch. "No Denying Link Between Athletes and Guns."

59. Joseph Williams. "Packed with Trouble: Mix of Athletes, Guns Is Problem." *Boston Globe*, December 23, 2008.

60. Quoted in Paul Hirsch. "When One Mistake Is a Gun Mistake Sports Careers Can Be Jeopardized." Free Library. www.the freelibrary.com/When+One+Mistake+Is+a+Gun+Mistake+ Sports+Careers+Can+Be+Jeopardized-a01074039570.

61. Imrem. "Does Violence in Sports Transfer to Homestead?"

62. Connie Chung. "Violent Athletes." *Good Morning America*, March 9, 1998.

63. Andrew SkinnerLopata. "Athletes Can Set Example on Domestic Violence." *Eugene (OR) Register Guard*, March 3, 2010.

64. Quoted in Chung. "Violent Athletes."

65. Quoted in Chung. "Violent Athletes."

66. SkinnerLopata. "Athletes Can Set Example on Domestic Violence."

67. Quoted in *Morning Edition*. "Violence in the Personal Lives of Amateur Athletes."

68. *Christian Science Monitor*. "Violence and the Culture of Star Athletes." February 7, 2000.

69. Quoted in Jerry Kirshenbaum. "An American Outrage." *Sports Illustrated*, February 27, 1989, p. 18.

70. Quoted in Jeff Rude. "It's a Start." *Golfweek*, February 26, 2010, p. 33.

71. Dan Jenkins. "Talk About Total Pressure." *Sports Illustrated*, June 27, 1977. http://sportsillustrated.cnn/com/vault/article/magazine/MAG1092539/index.

72. Mark Reason. "Michelle Wie Tells of Death Threat Dangers." *Telegraph* (UK), July 29, 2009. www.telegraph.co/uk/sport/golf/womensgolf/593391/Michelle-Wie-tells-of-death-threats.

73. Quoted in *Reason*. "Michelle Wie Tells of Death Threat Dangers."

74. Quoted in Aaron J. Lopez. "Prime Targets: Athletes Increasingly Aware Fame Can Result in Violence." *Rocky Mountain News* (Denver), December 29, 2007.

75. Samuel Bell Jr. "Violence and Sports: When Will It End?" *Bleacher Report*. September 2, 2008. http://bleacherreport.com/articles/53376-violence-and-sports-when-will-it-end.

Chapter 4: Violence by Nonathletes: Spectators, Coaches, and Parents

76. Nosotro. "Violence in Sports."

77. Jamieson and Orr. *Sport and Violence*, p. 120.

78. Quoted in Laura K. Egendorf, ed. *Sports and Athletes*. San Diego: Greenhaven, 1999, p. 15.

79. Gorman and Weeks. *Death at the Ballpark*, p. 146.

80. Quoted in Coakley. *Sports in Society*, p. 219.

81. *Cincinnati Post*. "Cleveland Fans Turn Violent." December 7, 2001.

82. Bruce Lowitt. "Disturbed Fan Stabs Top-Ranked Seles." *St. Petersburg (FL) Times*, October 7, 1999.

83. Quoted in "Crowd Psychology." AbsoluteAstronomy.com. www.absoluteastronomy.com/topics/Crowd_psychology.

84. Gorman and Weeks. *Death at the Ballpark*, p. 148.

85. Quoted in Coakley. *Sports in Society*, p. 222.

86. Engh. *Why Johnny Hates Sports*, p. 25.

87. Heather A. Dinich. "From Backers to Attackers: Parents Can Be Problems, Sometimes Violent Ones." *Washington Post*, July 26, 2000.

88. Dennis M. Docheff and James H. Conn. "It's No Longer a Spectator Sport: Eight Ways to Get Involved and Help Fight Parental Violence in Youth Sports." *Parks and Recreation*, March 1, 2004.

89. Quoted in *The O'Reilly Factor*. "Parent Accused of Violence at Youth Sports Event." Fox News Channel, September 8, 2006.

90. Engh. *Why Johnny Hates Sports*, p. 3.

91. Quoted in Mark Stewart. "Good Sports?" *Insight on the News*, June 19, 2000.

92. Jay Lovinger, ed. *The Gospel According to ESPN: Saints, Saviors, and Sinners*. New York: Hyperion, 2002, p. 80.

93. Lovinger. *The Gospel According to ESPN*, p. 83.

94. Quoted in Betsy Blaney, Associated Press. "Leach Gets Fired as Texas Tech Football Coach." *Salt Lake City Deseret News*, December 31, 2009.

95. Thomas Lake. "The Boy Who Died of Football." *Sports Illustrated*, December 6, 2010, p. 131.

96. "Jason Stinson Trial Aftermath." *Athletic Management*, September 25, 2009. www.athleticmanagement.com/2009/09/25/jason_stinson_trial_aftermath/index.php?printMe=1.

97. Thomas Lake. "The Boy Who Died of Football," p. 133.

Chapter 5: Reduction and Prevention of Violence in Sports

98. Quoted in Mark Stewart. "Good Sports?" *Insight on the News*, June 19, 2000.

99. Quoted in Rachel Blount. "Adult Violence in Youth Sports." *Minneapolis Star-Tribune*, January 2, 2007.

100. Quoted in John Feinstein. *A Season on the Brink*. New York: Simon and Schuster, 1989, p. 9.

101. Quoted in Williams. "Packed with Trouble."

102. Terry McDonell. "Staggered by the Impact." *Sports Illustrated*, November 1, 2010, p. 14.

103. Quoted in Mark Maske. "Goodell Will Stiffen Penalties for Illegal Hits." *Washington Post*, September 19, 2008.

104. Quoted in Tim Layden. "The Defender's View." *Sports Illustrated*, October 25, 2010, p. 38.

105. Quoted in Barry Wilner. "NFL to Start Suspending Players for Violent Hits." KOMO News.com, October 19, 2010. www .komonews.com/sports/professional/105280388.html.

106. Quoted in "NHL Players' Union Approves New Head Shot Ban." *USA Today*, March 26, 2010. www.usatoday.com/ sports/hockey/nhl/2010-03-25-head-shot-rule_N.htm.

107. Quoted in Dan O'Neill. "NHL Cracks Down on Hits to the Head." *St. Louis Dispatch*, March 25, 2010. www.stltoday .com/sports/hockey/professional/article_1d349039-1d33-51ce-a19b-95be6598fea3.html.

108. Coakley. *Sports in Society*, p. 207.

109. Quoted in Gorman and Weeks. *Death at the Ballpark*, p. 150.

110. Donald Collins. "Gun Violence at Youth Sports Contests: An Ever Present Threat in Urban Areas." MomsTeam. www .momsteam.com/team-of-experts/gun-violence-at-athletic-contests-an-administrators-nightmare.

111. *Christian Science Monitor*. "When Sports Violence Is a Criminal Act. February 28, 2000.

112. "When Sports Is a Criminal Act."

113. Quoted in "When Sports Is a Criminal Act."

114. Jackson Katz. "Mentors in Violence Prevention." Jackson Katz. www.jacksonkatz.com/aboutmvp.html.

115. Quoted in George Dohrmann and Jeff Benedict. "Rap Sheets, Recruits, and Repercussions." *Sports Illustrated*, March 7, 2011, p. 34.

116. Dohrmann and Benedict. "Rap Sheets, Recruits, and Repercussions, pp. 36–38.

Chapter 1: Violence in Sports—
Sanctioned and Unsanctioned

1. What is the earliest recorded example of violence in sports?
2. What is sanctioned violence? Why is it allowed?
3. What is unsanctioned violence?
4. How does unsanctioned violence differ from sport to sport? Give examples from at least three different sports.
5. What role might the media play in sports violence?

Chapter 2: Fostering Violence Through
Competition and Aggression

1. What is the winning-at-all-costs attitude?
2. How do fans impact violence in sports?
3. How does sport management impact violence in sports?
4. What is sports rage? Give two examples.
5. What is sportsmanship?

Chapter 3: The Spillover of Sports
Violence: Off-the-Field Violence

1. Is there a connection between on-the-field and off-the-field violence?
2. Why do some consider gun possession by an athlete a "disaster waiting to happen"? Give two examples.
3. What can happen when a collegiate athlete is accused of sexual assault? Why?
4. What is entitlement?

Chapter 4: Violence by Nonathletes: Spectators, Coaches, and Parents

1. What is hooliganism?
2. How do crowd mentality and alcohol affect spectator violence?
3. What is "parental rink rage" or "Little League parent syndrome"?
4. What role might the coach play in sports violence? Give two examples.

Chapter 5: Reduction and Prevention of Violence in Sports

1. What efforts are being made in youth sports to reduce sports violence?
2. What steps are professional sports leagues taking to control violence on the field of play? Is it effective?
3. What can be done to reduce spectator violence?
4. What is the role of the police in sports violence?
5. What are some ways to reduce off-the-field violence?

ORGANIZATIONS TO CONTACT

Canadian Centre for Ethics in Sport
350-955 Green Valley Crescent
Ottawa, ON K2C 3V4
Phone: (800) 672-7775
E-mail: info@cces.ca
Website: www.cces.ca

The Canadian Centre for Ethics in Sport is an organization dedicated to promoting drug-free sport, fair play, safety, and nonviolence.

Josephson Institute
9841 Airport Blvd., Ste. 300
Los Angeles, CA 90045
Phone: (800) 711-2670
Fax: (310) 846-4858
Website: http://josephsoninstitute.org

The Josephson Institute is an organization dedicated to the improvement of ethical standards in society.

National Alliance for Youth Sports
2050 Vista Pkwy.
West Palm Beach, FL 33411
Phone: (561) 681-1141
Fax: 561-684-2546
Website: www.nays.org

The National Alliance for Youth Sports is an organization that provides educational programs for young athletes, coaches, parents, and administrators.

National Coalition Against Violent Athletes
PO Box 62043
Littleton, CO 80162
Phone: (303) 524-9853
Website: http://ncava.org

The National Coalition Against Violent Athletes is an organization dedicated to providing support for women who have been victims of sexual assault at the hands of athletes. The coalition also provides educational material on the subject of crimes against women.

Northeastern University Center for the Study of Sport in Society
360 Huntington Ave., Ste. 510 INV
Boston, MA 02115
Phone: (617) 373-4025
Fax: (617) 373-4566
E-mail: sportinsociety@neu.edu
Website: www.northeastern.edu/sportinsocietty

The Northeastern University Center for the Study of Sport in Society is a research facility that studies sports in society and the issue of violence in sport.

Positive Coaching Alliance
Positive Coaching Group LLC
6107 Jerome Trail
Dallas, TX 75252
Phone: (927) 733-9963
Fax: (927) 733-4228
Website: www.positivecoach.org

The Positive Coaching Alliance is an organization that promotes positive coaching and provides tools for coaches and parents to enhance youth athletics.

FOR MORE INFORMATION

Books

Gilda Berger. *Violence and Sports*. New York: Franklin Watts, 1990. A comprehensive look at violence and sports.

Louise Gerdes, ed. *Violence*. Detroit: Greenhaven, 2008. A book that looks at the overall culture of violence.

Neil Reynolds. *Pain Gang: Pro Football's Fifty Toughest Players*. Washington, DC: Potomac, 2006. A look at some of the toughest and most violent football players in the National Football League.

Magazines and Journals

Lars Anderson. "Party Hard and Race Harder." *Sports Illustrated*, February 15, 2010. An article about violence in NASCAR.

Mark Bechtel. "The King, the Blizzard, the Crash and the Fight That Put NASCAR on the Map." *Sports Illustrated*, February 15, 2010. An article about violence in NASCAR.

David Epstein. "Speed: A Way of Life, and Death." *Sports Illustrated*, February 22, 2010. An article about NASCAR.

Jonathon Gatehouse. "Our National Blood Sport." *Maclean's*, May 25, 2009. The author examines the issue of violence in Canadian professional hockey.

Journal of Physical Education, Recreation, and Dance. "Parent Violence in Youth Sports." October 1, 2000. An article about parental violence in sports.

Peter King. "Concussions: The Hits That Are Changing Football." *Sports Illustrated*, November 1, 2010. An article about helmet-to-helmet hits and the increased number of concussions in professional football.

Pete Kotz. "Tough Guy." *Cleveland Scene*, October 19, 2000. An article about hockey's tough guys, or enforcers.

Robert Lipstye. "Brutality: Who Needs It?" *USA Today*, March 24, 2010. The author examines brutality and violence in sports.

Christopher Mains. "In Light of the Violence Occurring in Today's Society, Should Contact Sports Such as Football Have a Place in High School Athletic Contests?" *Journal of Physical Education, Recreation, and Dance*, August 1, 1996. An article examining violence in high school sports.

Jim Trotter. "Blow by Blow." *Sports Illustrated*, October 25, 2010. An article about the increased number of concussions in professional football due to helmet-to-helmet hits.

Newspapers

Albany (NY) Times Union. "Fan Violence." November 21, 2004. A list of incidents involving fans and violence.

Coventry Evening Telegraphy (England). "History of Violence." September 24, 2001. An article relating some of the violence that occurs in soccer.

Kevin Paul Dupont and Larry Tye. "Another Victim: Assault of Kerrigan the Latest Example of Spreading Violence in the Sports World." *Boston Globe*, January 7, 1994. An article about the assault of figure skater Nancy Kerrigan and the increase in violence against athletes.

Bob Molinaro. "Beanballs Have No Place in Baseball." *Virginian-Pilot* (Norfolk, VA), September 29, 2007. An article about baseball violence.

Brandon Ringler. "Modern Baseball Turns to Violence." University Wire, July 11, 2003. An article about violence in baseball.

Ross Smith. "Action Urged over Football Violence." *Journal* (Newcastle, England), April 6, 2007. An article about violence in soccer.

Chris Snow. "National Hockey League: Looking for Source of Hockey Violence." *Minneapolis Star-Tribune*, March 14, 2004. An article about violence in ice hockey.

Rick Telander. "Was Frank Robinson's Ruling Too Harsh?" *Chicago Sun Times*, April 28, 2000. The author contends that violence has no place in sports.

Jeff Ziegler. "Violence and Sports, Coaches Need to Set a Good Example." *Virginian-Pilot* (Norfolk, VA), March 16, 1997. An article about coaches setting a good example for their players in regard to violence.

Internet Sources

Clair Alvies. "Nine Recommendations to Reduce Sports Violence." *Self Help Magazine*, January 29, 2010. www.selfhelp magazine.com/article/sports-violence. An article about recommendations to decrease violence in sports.

Associated Press, "Former NFL Running Back Phillips Sentenced in LA to Prison." October 3, 2008. http://sports.espn.go.com/nfl/story?id=3624420. An article about off-the-field violence.

William McCall. "Instant Replay Official Gets Death Threat, Considers Resigning." *Seattle Times*, September 19, 2006. www.seattletimes.nwsource.com/html/sports/2003265232_webref19.html. An article about violence directed at referees.

Eddie Pells. "Green Recalls Life-and-Death 1977 Win." *USA Today*, August 12, 2007. www.usatoday.com/sports/golf/2007-08-12-935384912_x.htm. An article about death threats against athletes.

Penn State Live. "Sports Machismo May Be Cue to Teen Violence." January 23, 2008. http://live.psu.edu/story/28254. An article about the relationship between sports machismo and violence.

Clay Travis. "Time to Get Serious on Death Threats." Fanhouse, June 1, 2009. http://ncaafootball.fanhouse.com/2009/06/01/time-to-get-serious-on-death-threats. A senior National Collegiate Athletic Association writer shares his opinion about what should be done about death threats to athletes.

Websites

Little League Organization (www.littleleague.org). This is the official website for Little League Baseball.

Major League Baseball (www.mlb.com). This is the official website for Major League Baseball.

National Association for Stock Car Auto Racing (www.nascar.com). This is the official website for sports car racing.

National Basketball Association (www.nba.com). This is the official website for the National Basketball Association.

National Football League (www.nfl.com). This is the official website for professional football.

National Hockey League (www.nhl.com). This is the official website for professional ice hockey.

Pop Warner (www.popwarner.com). This is the official website for youth football leagues.

INDEX

PICTURE CREDITS

ABOUT THE AUTHOR

Anne Wallace Sharp is the author of the adult book *Gifts*; several children's books, including *Daring Pirate Women*; and eighteen other titles for Lucent Books. She has also written numerous magazine articles for both adults and juveniles. A retired registered nurse, Sharp has a degree in history. Her interests include reading, traveling, and spending time with her grandchildren, Jacob and Nicole. She is also an avid sports fan. Sharp lives in Beavercreek, Ohio.